———————

Series Story Editor **Mary Ann Cooper** is
America's foremost soap opera expert. She
writes the nationally syndicated column
Speaking of Soaps, is a major contributor to
soap opera magazines, and has appeared on
numerous radio and television talk shows.

Author **Nicole Brooks** lives with her
husband and daughter on the west coast.
Between novels she relaxes at her mountain
cabin and catches up on her favorite soap
operas.

From the editor's desk...

Dear Friend,

Captivating ... delightful ... heartwarming ... these are but a few of the enthusiastic comments we've received from Soaps & Serials readers. We're delighted. Every month the fine team of writers and editors at Pioneer pool all their resources to bring you seven new spectacular books.

Based on actual scripts from DAYS OF OUR LIVES, each novel is written with you in mind. As we recreate the plot and characters of DAYS OF OUR LIVES, we strive to capture the feeling and tone of the show. We can thank our story editor, Mary Ann Cooper, for her sharp attention to details and her genuine love for each and every show.

It's contagious—and we want you to share the spirit! Tell us more about you. How long have you been a fan of DAYS OF OUR LIVES? What other daytime and prime time shows do you watch? How long have you been reading Soaps & Serials?

Keep in touch! And don't miss the special surprise from Mary Ann Cooper in next month's books!

For Soaps & Serials,

Rosalind Noonan

Rosalind Noonan
Editor-in-Chief
Pioneer Communications Network, Inc.

P.S. If you missed previous volumes of DAYS OF OUR LIVES and can't find them in your local book source, please see the order form inserted in this book.

DAYS OF OUR LIVES

9

FRIENDS AND LOVERS

PIONEER COMMUNICATIONS NETWORK, INC.

Friends and Lovers

DAYS OF OUR LIVES paperback novels are published and distributed by Pioneer Communications Network, Inc.

SOAPS & SERIALS™ is a trademark of Pioneer Communications Network, Inc.

ISBN: 0-916217-59-0

Printed in Canada

10 9 8 7 6 5 4 3 2 1

FRIENDS AND LOVERS

Chapter One

Starting Over

The night air was cool and damp. Michael Horton inhaled deeply, slowly expelling his breath. The decision had been made. He was on his own.

Headlights shone over the slight rise in the road behind him. Ignoring all his parents' warnings about hitchhiking he stopped, planted himself defiantly at the side of the road, and stuck out his thumb.

The car zoomed by, its taillights quickly fading to a red blur. Hitching up his backpack, Michael kept walking. It didn't matter. He had no particular place to go. A ride would have just gotten him there faster.

With a twinge of conscience, he thought how his mother would feel when she found him gone. But it was just too bad. She'd been the one who'd turned from his father. It was her fault he'd gone off and married someone else. Her fault and Bill's. The blame was all theirs.

Kicking a stone out of his path, Michael fed his anger, glad his mother and Bill would suffer. Their love for each other was wrong. *Wrong!*

Bill was his father's brother, for God's sake. How could he do that? How could he steal his brother's wife and feel no remorse? It was sick. Sick and wrong. And the only reason his father had left and gone back to that other woman was because he'd felt so betrayed—not because he couldn't remember who he was.

At least that's what Michael wanted to believe. He couldn't accept that his father had left him behind. He had to blame someone. His father's amnesia couldn't be just a quirk of fate; he couldn't accept that. It was his mother's fault, he reasoned with all the conviction of hot-tempered adolescence. His mother's and Bill's. But just wait until they woke up and found him gone.

He walked on, several more miles, buoyed by his sense of vengeance. Only when dawn was turning the horizon to a soft pink did his weariness return. *They wouldn't care*, he thought miserably, shoulders drooping. They would probably just dust their hands and say, "Too bad. Oh, well. Michael's gone. Good riddance."

Salem's city skyline was little more than a gray outline hidden by the soft, drizzling rain when Michael finally stopped to look back. He was on the far outskirts of town, on a winding road that followed the riverfront. Gritting his teeth, he told himself to forget his mother and father and everyone else. He was on his own. And he was going to make it.

There was a gas station up ahead. It was still closed, but the hours were posted on a cardboard sign hanging on the inside of the dirt-spattered glass door. 7:00 A.M. He'd wait until they opened and get himself a Coke from the vending machine. Then he'd figure out just where he was going.

Settling down on the asphalt, Michael adjusted his backpack behind his head and leaned against the wall. Hardly a car drove by. This was the old road into town, used before the highway was built, and now traveled mostly by sightseers or the people who lived near the riverfront.

He closed his eyes, felt the aching weariness in his muscles, and fell fast asleep.

Susan Peters was dancing. Lighter than air, she twirled and twisted, her pale blue chiffon skirt billowing around her, feathery as a cloud. She could dance forever.

The ballroom was deserted. Alone, she executed perfect turns, one upon another, as clean and pure as any prima ballerina. It was heaven! She would never stop dancing. Never, never, never.

She paused for breath beside one of the doric columns and there he was—that mystery man who always came to dance with her.

"I know you," he said, taking her hand, and then they were dancing together.

There was a thrill to these clandestine meetings Susan found addictive. *If Greg ever finds out he'll divorce me*, she thought, but then she was in her lover's arms. She could hear his breathing, could touch his shirt, could feel the hard strength of his arms around her.

"Susan, Susan," he murmured, but his voice made her feel uneasy.

She struggled to understand, just as she struggled to hold on to him. She was reaching, reaching, reaching . . . and then she woke up to find Greg's arm thrown over her waist, Greg's lips murmuring her name.

Instantly, she felt depressed. *It was only a dream.* There was no lover, only Greg, and he wasn't even awake. She supposed she should be glad it was her name he whispered in his sleep, but instead she just felt frustrated and angry. *Why, oh why, was life so unfair?*

"Susan?" Greg passed a hand over his eyes and yawned. "What're you doing?"

"Nothing. I just woke up."

"You were reaching for me. I thought maybe . . ." He trailed off, giving her a look from beneath his lashes.

"What?" She threw back the covers, then waited, wishing for something she couldn't quite name. If only Greg were different, more eager, perhaps. Then maybe her insecurities would disappear.

"Never mind. I just thought you were in the mood for a little lovemaking, that's all."

"Why does it always have to be me? Don't you ever want to make love?"

Greg's eyes opened wider. "Are you kidding?" he asked in astonishment.

"Well, then, act like it!" Susan said, angry all over again. In a huff she stalked to the bathroom and savagely brushed her hair until it crackled. She looked at her reflection, checking for any signs of age. No, she still looked younger than she was, she thought with relief.

After turning on the shower, Susan stripped off her nightgown, then stood under the needle-sharp spray. Closing her eyes, she let the hot water pour over her skin, soothe away her frustrations. Lately, she'd felt even more restless and unhappy than usual. She thought she'd gotten past all that, but apparently she hadn't. Years had come and gone, and nothing had changed for her and Greg. Maybe it never would.

And it was all because of Eric, she thought bitterly. Eric, and that damn book of his. It was bad enough that she'd had to admit to herself—and to Greg—that she hadn't been raped by the stranger in the park. It had been a willing act on her part. An act committed before she'd met Greg and fallen in love with him. Yet, to add insult to injury, the stranger had been Greg's brother, Eric, a novelist, who'd revealed the whole awful truth in his thinly veiled story, *In His Brother's Shadow*. Not even her miscarriage of the baby conceived that night had stopped Eric, or made him show any pity.

Mentally shuddering, Susan turned off the shower. She could still remember how people had treated her afterwards; everyone in Salem had been privy to her innermost secrets. That Greg had married her anyway had been a testimony to his love, yet things had never been quite the same. Now, years later, the seed of mistrust that had been sown was still growing, flourishing, and Susan felt frustrated and restless and tired of all the unspoken blame and suspicion.

Maybe it was time for a change.

"Susan?" Greg tapped his knuckles against the bathroom door.

"I'll be out in a minute."

"Well, hurry. I've got to be at the hospital by seven."

The hospital. Susan made a moue with her lips as she toweled off. She'd thought it would be fun being married to a doctor. The prestige, the parties, the money! But all it amounted to was endless work, calls in the middle of the night, no time for any fun. And if Greg wasn't at the hospital, he was at the offices he shared with Dr. Neil Curtis. Her life was slipping by her and she had nothing to show for it!

She slid past Greg without a look in his direction. "What did I do now?" she heard him mutter just before the bathroom door shut behind him.

Nothing! You've done nothing! she wanted to scream. Then, before she could scream out something nasty and unforgivable that would only make matters worse, she pulled on some slacks and a silk blouse and went downstairs to make herself a cup of coffee.

"Hey, son. What're ya doin' here?"

A strong hand shook Michael roughly. It took a second or two for him to wake up, and when he did he was alarmed to see a bearded, sun-wrinkled face staring down at him.

"Ah asked you a question," the man said, his lower lip stuffed with snuff.

"I—I fell asleep. I wasn't doing anything."

"That right?" The man swept a quick eye over the pumps, as if he'd expected them to have been tampered with. Then he narrowed his gaze back on Michael. "Then get outta here," he said. "G'on now. I gotta get to work."

"Is this your service station?" Michael stood up, dusting dirt off the seat of his pants.

"What if it is?"

"I just wanted to get a Coke out of the vending machine."

The man gave him a long look. "Why ain't you in school?"

"I finished school," Michael lied, following after him as he unlocked the door. Fishing in his pockets, Michael found some change and dropped it into the machine. He opened the bottle and took a long swallow, then wiped his mouth with the back of his hand.

The man was opening the cash drawer. He wasn't as old as he'd originally thought, Michael realized, putting the man's age between fifty and sixty. He just had a stooped back and obviously didn't pay much attention to his appearance.

A plan began to form hazily in the back of Michael's mind. "You run this place by yourself?" he asked.

"Yep."

"Don't you have anybody working for you?"

"Nope. Don't want no one either. Last kid I hired stole me blind."

"You mean, you do all the work yourself?"

"That a crime?"

"No, I just . . ." Sighing, Michael shrugged. "I just thought you might need some help."

"You a runaway, kid?"

"No." His answer was swift, too swift, he realized, as the older fellow's eyes gleamed.

"You're a runaway," he said, nodding his head and shooting a stream of tobacco juice accurately into a corroded brass spittoon.

Michael would have liked to argue, but he could see there was no point. "Okay, I left home. But I'm going to finish high school. I just couldn't live with them anymore."

The older man nodded.

"I need a job," Michael said, laying all his cards on the table. "I was going to get out of Salem altogether but I don't know. If I get a job and my own place, there's not a whole lot they can do about it."

"They can haul your bones into juvenile court, kid. Don't think they can't."

"But they won't. My mother's a psychiatrist. Believe me, she'd try to work things out another way."

"So why're you runnin' away?"

"My stepfather." Michael's face changed. Whenever he thought about Bill it was all he could do to keep from slamming his fist into a wall. Bill had tried to usurp Michael's father's position in the household, not only with Laura, his mother, but with him as well. Bill had acted for all the world as if he were Michael's only father, and that Mickey Horton had never existed. But Mickey was Michael's father. And Bill was an imposter. Michael hated laying claim to Bill even as his uncle.

"Can't hire no underage runaway," the man said. "Sorry."

"I'd work extra hard. You wouldn't even have to report my wages."

"You're a smart kid, ain't ya?" The man gave him another searching look, then wiped his greasy palm on his overalls and stuck out a hand. "Name's Lou. Y'wanna job?" He jerked his head in the direction of the pumps. "Show me just how bad."

Eagerly, Michael followed Lou outside, listening to all his directions. When a car pulled in for gas, Michael was left on his own to deal with the customer. After the sale was made, Lou gave a grunt of satisfaction and told him he could stay for the day.

The hours flew by. Michael was given a half

hour for lunch and he used the time to walk to a small cafe down the road, bolt down a sandwich, and hurry back. By the time his shift was over he'd learned how to change a tire, check the oil, fill the tank, take a credit card sale, and a million and a half other things.

As Lou counted out his pay, Michael waited, wondering if he had a job for the next day. His hopes sank as Lou said nothing. He'd actually turned away and reached for his backpack when the older man said, "Help that car just pullin' in, then be back here tomorrow at seven on the nose."

"You got it!" Michael yelled, dropping his pack and running to the silver Lincoln Continental idling at the pumps. Jubilation filled him. He had a job! Now all he needed was a place to live.

"Fill it up, please," a tremulous feminine voice said.

Michael looked in the window. The girl wasn't much older than he was, if at all. She was blond and petite, with pretty blue eyes. But those eyes were red now and twin tracks of tears were running down her cheeks. She turned away, vainly trying to conceal the fact that she was crying.

"Uh, sure," Michael said. "Regular or super?"

"Regular."

"Want me to check the oil?"

She looked at him helplessly and before he could stop himself, Michael asked, "Are you all right? I mean, would you like a Coke or something? I could get you one."

"Thanks, no." She shook her head, managing a smile. "I'm just—having a bad day."

"Hey, listen, I know what those are like." He gave her an encouraging smile, then grabbed a red rag and a squeeze bottle of window cleaner. He could see her as he sprayed the windshield. *Man, she sure was pretty!*

"Excuse me." She stuck her head out the side window. "Were you serious about that Coke?"

"Sure. I'll get you one."

"Here"—she started digging in her purse—"let me get you some change."

"Forget it. My pleasure." Michael stuffed the rag in his back pocket and went to the vending machine. He came back with a chilled bottle, then had to argue to keep her from paying him.

"I'm Trish Clayton," she introduced herself shyly. "I don't think I've seen you here before."

"Michael Horton," he answered, then wondered if he should have been more discreet. He was going to have to be careful if he didn't want his mother and Bill to find him. "I just started work today. You come through here often?"

"Not that often. Sometimes. When I get the car." She stared moodily through the windshield. "It's my parents'."

She paid in cash and Michael murmured a thank-you and good-bye. To his surprise, she pulled the Lincoln to the side and stepped out. In a pair of tight jeans and a loose pullover sweater, her hair swinging to her shoulders, she looked ten times more sophisticated than he did. Or at least that's how Michael felt as he nervously watched her approach.

"I hope you don't mind. I just didn't want to—go home yet. Did you just move here, or something?"

"Yeah."

"Do you go to school? How old are you?"

Michael swallowed. This was going to kill it for sure. "I'm a senior. In high school." He shrugged. *What the hell*, he figured. *Might as well go for broke.* "I just left home. Couldn't stand it."

Trish's eyes widened. "No kidding. Wow. I wish I had the guts to do that."

"Why?"

"Oh . . ." She made a deprecatory sound. "Reasons. You know."

He didn't know, exactly, but he heard in Trish's words an echo of his own unhappy home life. Sensing the topic was getting too sticky, Michael shifted the conversation and soon they were talking about school. He learned Trish was a senior, too, and that she had dreams of being a fashion designer when she got out of school. Michael didn't know what he wanted to be. He'd thought he would follow in his father's footsteps and become a lawyer once, but now . . . well, circumstances had changed his mind.

With a gasp, Trish looked at her watch. "I've got to get back or they'll kill me!" She glanced up at Michael. "Are you, er, going to be here tomorrow?"

"Uh-huh."

"If I'm by this way, I'll stop in."

"Great. Maybe we could get a burger and fries somewhere," Michael invited recklessly. A little voice inside his head told him to save his money, but another argued that he needed all the friends he could get.

Trish smiled, and all his misgivings faded away. "I'll make a point of it, then," she said, then she waved and walked back to her car.

Michael watched her pull away. He saw Lou turn off the lights, climb into his pickup, lift a hand, and drive off, too. With a sense of shock he realized he'd just watched the only friends he had drive away.

"You sleep in your clothes, kid?" Lou asked, critically checking Michael over from head to toe.

Hiding a yawn, Michael thought that Lou shouldn't be one to talk. The man looked like a derelict. "I slept outside last night," he admitted. "I haven't got a place yet."

"Then you'd best get one. Else you'll scare off the customers."

Half-amused, Michael took care of the desultory traffic that came through the service station. Thinking of Trish, he tried to clean himself up a bit in the restroom, and realized he was going to have to find a place to live right away.

She arrived right on schedule, just as Michael was getting paid. Lou looked at the silver Lincoln and shook his grizzled head. "Be careful with that one."

"Trish?" Michael bristled. To him, she was a goddess. He didn't need Lou talking down about her.

"Her parents," Lou said wisely. "They come through once in a while. Wouldn't want to cross her old man."

"Why?"

Lou expertly shot into his spittoon. "Just don't think it'd be a smart idea."

"I've got the car for an hour," Trish said brightly, and Lou went inside the garage. "Climb in. We can go to Harvey's."

Michael diffidently sat down in the passenger side, conscious of his dusty jeans against the gray leather seats. But Trish ignored his discomfiture and soon they were pulling into a burger stand with HARVEY'S BURGERS burned into an oak board and nailed across a weathered shack. Inside, however, the place was spotless, with red-and-white checked tablecloths thrown over rough wooden tables.

"I didn't know this was here," Michael said.

"You're not from Salem, then."

"Well, yes, I am. But I lived closer in, over that way," he said, gesturing vaguely.

"The rich side of town?" Trish asked, her brows raising. "My stepfather wants to move there. He bought the Lincoln and now he wants a new place to go with it."

"You have a stepfather?" Michael seized on this piece of information.

"Yes." Trish instantly went silent. Then after a long, uncomfortable moment, she said, "He likes people to think he's my father, but he's not."

"You don't like him?"

"Oh, he's okay." Trish buried her nose in the menu.

"I hate my stepfather," Michael said. "I really do."

Trish slowly raised her eyes. "Is that why you left home?"

"Mostly. There were other reasons."

"Where are you staying now?"

"Nowhere." Michael made a face. "Can't you tell?"

"I know of a place," she said, slowly, as if thinking through her thoughts. "It's a little apartment not far from here, near the riverfront. It's old and every once in a while the plumbing backs up, but it's cheap. You can stay there, no questions asked."

"How do you know?" Michael asked curiously.

"A girlfriend of mine moved in there for a while. She was having problems at home, too. But she moved back with her parents a couple of months ago."

"I'm never moving back," Michael stated firmly.

The waitress came and took their order and soon they were delivered burger baskets filled with the biggest burgers Michael had ever seen. He did a quick calculation of his money left and decided he was safe.

Trish munched on a french fry. "I'd love to have my own place," she said, sighing. "I'm going to be eighteen soon and I can't wait to move out."

"Move in with me," Michael said, grinning. "We'll share expenses."

"I wish."

"I'm serious. No strings attached. I'm broke and I don't have a friend anywhere near here."

Trish smiled wistfully. "You've got me," she said, and Michael felt warm inside. Things were working out.

He paid for their burgers though Trish argued valiantly. "If you expect me to move in with you expenses are split right down the middle, buddy," she said lightly. But when Michael pounced eagerly on her commitment to get a place with him, she changed the subject.

Later that evening, however, Trish drove Michael by the apartment complex. It was run-

down, with a weed-choked central lawn that
served all ten apartments. The empty one was
on the end.

Trish led the way to it and Michael looked
through the windows. From what he could see,
it was just what he needed. Calling on his courage, he knocked on the manager's door, which
was opened by a tired-looking woman in rollers.
She had him sign his name and age.

"You sure you're eighteen?" she asked, nar-
rowing her eyes.

"Yes," Michael lied.

Shrugging, she pulled down the key, then
demanded payment up front for the entire
month. It was Trish who explained he'd just gotten a job, Trish who convinced her to accept the
money Michael had and put him up for a few
days, at least until he could get some more cash
together.

When it was over and Michael was standing
in the center of his one-bedroom apartment,
looking about him in dazed delight, Trish came
and gave him a quick hug. "Good luck, friend,"
she said softly, then headed out the door.

Michael was left with the scent of her sweet
perfume filling his head and the warm memory
of her cheek brushing his.

Greg Peters flipped through his appointment
book, feeling restless and frustrated. Susan had
barely spoken to him for two days. What had he
done that was so terrible? Nothing, she'd said.
So why the cold shoulder?

It was so typical of Susan, he thought angrily.
These days all she did was complain. No matter
how hard he tried to get close to her, he always

ended up saying or doing the wrong thing.

After penciling in several appointments that
Roxie, Curtis's and Peters's receptionist, had
given him, Greg pulled his jacket off his oak
coatrack and swept all the paraphernalia off his
desk, wadding up scraps of paper and tossing
them into the waste can. He might as well
leave, he reasoned. Coming in on his day off
hadn't worked. Nothing worked.

In the hallway, he overheard voices coming
from Dr. Neil Curtis's office, Greg's associate at the
clinic. Neil was trying to console a woman client,
but through the partially opened doorway Greg
could hear the way her voice quivered and broke as
she spoke. Feeling uncomfortable eavesdropping,
he turned to leave, but at that moment Neil and the
woman stepped into the hall.

"Stop worrying," Neil was saying to her.
"There's nothing to worry about."

"But I don't want—" She cut herself off when
she saw Greg, her lips parting in dismay.
Quickly, the hands that had been clutching
Neil's arm dropped to her sides. Though she
tried to hide it, Greg could see the way her fingers trembled as she curled them into fists and
tried to stuff them into the pockets of her mink-
trimmed coat.

"Well, hello, Greg," Neil said, surprised.
"What are you doing here? This isn't your day
at the office."

"I just had to pick up a few things. I was going to
the Racquet Club anyway and decided I might as
well swing by." Greg's gaze drifted back to the
blond woman. She had classic features and a
strangely touching vulnerability. By her clothes
and hair he guessed she was one of Neil's wealthier

patients, but he'd never seen her before.

Expecting to be introduced, he was surprised when Neil hustled the woman out the side door and said, "I'll call you tomorrow. Don't build mountains out of molehills, now. Your tests all came back fine."

"New patient?" Greg asked when Neil returned.

"Yeah." He turned to his office.

"What's she suffering from?"

"Look, Greg, I don't have time to discuss her case with you. Besides, she wants it kept strictly private. It's nothing really, anyway; she's mainly a hypochondriac."

"Neil . . ."

"Catch me tomorrow, hmm?" Neil gave him a forced smile just before he closed the door to his office.

Perplexed, Greg stared after him. Then he shook his head and let himself into the cool fall afternoon.

Neil slowly let out his breath. Amanda Howard. The woman was a mass of nerves. He hadn't expected that. She'd seemed so cool and untouchable when he'd first met her, as unruffled as a quiet summer lake, but underneath . . . His mind boggled just thinking about the complicated woman he'd uncovered. And he'd had to lie to Greg and pretend she was seeing him as a patient.

Crossing to his desk, Neil picked up his phone. There were calls he needed to make. Personal calls. Calls Amanda had interrupted.

"Hello, Jimmy?" His fingers did a nervous dance on his desktop. "It's Neil Curtis. Listen,

I've taken care of that little problem. No, everything's okay. I'll meet you tomorrow night at the usual place, okay? Okay. See you then."

Replacing the receiver, Neil was annoyed to see his palms were sweating. He wiped them on his lab coat, his fingers accidentally encountering his name pin. Unhooking it, he stared at the name. DR. NEIL CURTIS.

A lump grew in his throat. *How had he ever gotten into so much trouble?*

Michael turned up the collar of his jacket, fighting back the chilly breeze that made the tips of his ears bright red. He was cold all the time, but he wasn't interested in turning the heat up in his apartment. Frugality was his middle name these days. He'd turned the heat register to off this morning before he'd come to work.

While he stamped his feet and blew on his fingers, he heard the wheeze and rattle of some kind of vehicle coming around the corner. Looking up, he saw a dilapidated old Ford pull into the pumps, its tailpipe belching black smoke.

"Fill 'er up?" he asked, looking at the young man behind the wheel.

"Just give me a couple dollars' worth," the man answered. He was around twenty, with dark brown hair and an aristocratic nose. But his hair hung to his shoulders, and there was a world-weary slant to his mouth.

As Michael worked the gasoline pump, he couldn't help looking at him time and time again. There was something familiar about him. It seemed like he'd met him before. But where? Was he from Salem? He must be. Michael searched his memory and came up blank.

There was a girl in the car with him. She could be pretty, he decided, except her mouth was pulled down in a perpetual frown of displeasure. Her hair was long and dark and hung in lank strings over her shoulders. Michael caught her eye just as she took a long drag on a cigarette. Seeing him, she blew the smoke at the windshield where he was and turned away.

When the transaction was over and the car pulled out of the station, Michael gave up trying to figure out who they were. He had enough problems of his own to work out, not the least being that his landlord was going to demand the rest of his rent at the end of the week.

He hoped Lou would pay him enough to make it.

"He was kinda cute," Brooke Hamilton said, looking out the back window as they pulled away. She gave a sideways glance to David, hoping he might be jealous.

"He was just a kid."

"Yeah, but already he's got muscles. Did you see his shoulders?" She sighed expressively, then was piqued when David didn't pick up on the conversation. He'd been so different since they'd gotten close to Salem, she fumed. It had been better while they were still in Ash Grove, even though she'd had to put up with her mother, Adele. If it weren't for David's inheritance just sitting here waiting for him, she'd have refused to come.

Thinking of the money, Brooke forgot her anger. She leaned her head on David's shoulder and smiled to herself. David Banning. He was her ticket to heaven.

Chapter Two

Remember Me?

David flexed his fingers around the steering wheel and took a deep breath. He was here. Back in Salem. It seemed like a lifetime ago since he'd driven through these familiar streets.

"What are you thinking about?" Brooke asked, smiling up at him.

"Nothing." David wrapped his arm over her shoulder. He didn't want to have to admit there were butterflies in his stomach. Brooke wouldn't understand. She had nothing but contempt for her own mother. She couldn't possibly understand how he would feel about confronting his again.

His mother. David pictured her in his mind, remembering how young she'd seemed, how beautiful. Julie Anderson. There had been bad feelings when he'd left, angry feelings. He still resented her for being in love with Doug Williams instead of his adopted father, Scott Banning. Even after Scott's death she'd still carried a torch until Doug ended up marrying Julie's mother, Addie.

At least that had kept her from marrying Williams, David thought darkly. Since then he'd heard she'd married some guy by the name of Anderson—Bob Anderson. It had to be an improvement.

But what did he care anyway? He didn't want to see his mother. All he wanted was his inheritance—his rightful inheritance from his father's estate—and even though he wasn't quite twenty-one yet, he deserved the money now. All he had to do was convince his mother.

Wincing a little, David felt the butterflies return. He hated having to face willful, independent Julie Olson Anderson. It was a crying shame she had control of his money.

But all that was going to change.

"You know what I want," Brooke said dreamily, stroking his arm. "I want to move to the West Coast. What do you think? After we get your inheritance we could move to California, soak up the sun, live like royalty. Just you and me."

"Yeah. One step at a time, though," David said repressively.

"You don't think your mother'll give us any trouble, do you?" she asked, intuitively guessing his thoughts.

"Nah. She's a pushover. She'll give me what I want."

"What we both want." Brooke snuggled in closer. "You know, I'm almost looking forward to meeting her."

David made a sound between a snort and a laugh. *That makes one of us.*

Hating himself for the anxiety he felt, he glanced down at the address for Mr. and Mrs. Bob Anderson of Anderson Construction Company that he'd ripped from the pages of a local phone book. *The money's owed to me*, he reminded himself again. *It's mine. And nobody's going to keep it from me.*

Laura Horton pulled off her glasses and massaged her eyes. They felt gritty with lack of sleep. A week of no sleep, to be exact. Ever since she'd woken up to find her son's bed hadn't been slept in.

Where was Michael? She was worried sick about him. She'd known he'd been devastated when Mickey had come back to town and hadn't even recognized him, but so had they all. And she'd warned Michael that Mickey had been suffering from amnesia, but still he'd set himself up for a fall, expecting his father to remember him anyway.

Laura sighed. The terrible irony of it all was that Mickey wasn't Michael's natural father. Bill Horton was. And he was the one man Michael swore he hated above all others. What an awful truth! Michael's stepfather was in truth his biological father, and there was no way she could tell him!

She and Bill had discussed the problem often enough, each yearning for their son to learn the truth. Once, she'd even tried telling Michael. But he'd closed his ears, refused to listen. He'd never wanted to hear anything positive about Bill.

Michael, where are you?

With shaking hands, Laura reached for the phone. She should have called the police as soon as she'd realized he was missing. But she'd been so certain he would come home. What was he living on? He had no money. And he'd only taken a few clothes and some prized possessions.

"Yes, I'd like the number for the Salem Police Department," she said when the operator answered. She copied it down. "Thank you."

Now all she had to do was call.

"Dr. Horton?" Laura heard the tap on her office door, then saw her receptionist's head peek around. "There's someone here to see you."

Michael! Laura half-rose, heart pounding. Then reality set in. Her receptionist would recognize Michael. It had to be someone else. "Who is it?"

"She didn't give her name."

Laura glanced at the clock. There was still half an hour until her next appointment, but seeing this woman would delay her call to the police. Glad to seize upon any excuse, she said, "Send her in."

A few moments later a stylish blond woman Laura guessed to be in her early thirties stepped cautiously into her office. She was dressed in a taupe suit accented with a British green blouse, and several gold chains hung from her neck. Her earrings were gold, too, as was the diamond-studded watch she nervously checked as she settled herself in an opposite chair.

"My name's Amanda Howard," she said in a voice so low Laura could barely hear it.

"It's nice to meet you. I'm Dr. Laura Horton." Smiling, she extended a hand and noticed how cold the woman's was. "Did someone refer you to me?"

"No. No." Her fingers twisted the gold chains. "At the hospital, I overheard them saying how good you are, and I just took a chance . . ."

"At the hospital?" Laura's curiosity was piqued in spite of herself.

"My husband is sick. He's been having chest pains, heart trouble, you know. And I've been spending a lot of time at the hospital. They say he'll be fine but, oh, I don't know."

"You're worried you aren't hearing the whole truth," Laura put in kindly.

"No! It's not—no, that's not—what I mean is—" She made a sound of anguish, then collected herself. "It's me," she said on a deep sigh. "Sometimes, I almost wish he wouldn't get well. Isn't that terrible!"

"No." Laura regarded the distressed woman through reassuring eyes. "Everyone has those same types of feelings from time to time. Don't punish yourself. They'll pass."

"But it's not right. Charles has been good to me, better than he should be. And all I can think about is divorcing him and starting a new life!"

On the heels of this admission she rose to her feet, and Laura stood up, too, seeking to calm her. Unbeknownst to Amanda, she'd been through a very similar situation in her own life. "Please, Mrs. Howard, sit down. If you're unhappy in your marriage, the fact that your husband is sick isn't going to change that. *You're* going to have to. Either by working things out, or getting a divorce. When he's better—"

"That's the problem. I don't think he'll ever be better! He'll just stay the same and nothing will change." Her cheeks flushed. "I'm sorry I took up your time, Dr. Horton," she said, pulling on her gloves. "No one can help me. Please, please don't discuss this with anyone else."

"My patients' cases are all kept confidential."

"I know." Amanda let out a shaky sigh. "I know. But it was a mistake coming here. I wish . . ." She shook her head. "Thank you again, Dr. Horton."

"Wait." Laura came around her desk and followed her to reception.

Amanda stopped near the front desk. "What's your fee?" she asked, looking agitatedly around.

"There's no fee. This wasn't strictly an office visit, it was more an initial meeting. I'd like to talk with you again."

"No." Her smile was tight. "Really. Thank you, but I'll be fine. Here"—she pulled a fifty-dollar bill out of her wallet—"please let me know if that's not enough."

"No, it's fine," Laura said lamely. She felt an urgency to help Amanda but everything she said just seemed to drive the woman further and further away.

Amanda swept out of the office before Laura could offer another objection, and as the door whispered shut, Laura and her receptionist looked at one another in bafflement.

With a feeling she'd let something monumental slip through her fingers, Laura went back into her office, stared at the phone, picked up the receiver, then dropped it back in its cradle. Give him some slack, she told herself. A little more time and Michael will come home on his own.

Trying not to brood, she wrote notes to herself about Amanda Howard. The lady just might change her mind and come back—at least that's what Laura hoped for. It was clear to her that Amanda needed some serious psychiatric counseling.

* * *

Michael wiped off the scarred kitchen table with a dish towel, then looked around his apartment with pride. This was his place. All his own. Nobody else's.

If he could only afford it.

Grimacing, he looked in the cupboards. He'd had to be extra careful on his trip to the grocery store; he'd had less than three dollars. A can of soup and a loaf of bread and a half gallon of milk—those were his staples. Maybe he could talk Lou into working more hours, keeping the station open longer. That could bring in some extra income.

He jumped at the rap on his door, then his heart lifted as he realized it had to be Trish.

"Well, hello there," she said, when he opened the door. She was peering at him from between two large grocery sacks. "Can I come in?"

"Sure. Especially if you brought food. I thought I was going to die of canned-fooditis. What is this stuff?"

"The makings for spaghetti." Trish laughed as he threw a hand over his heart and fell across the table. "Don't expect too much. I'm not that great of a cook."

"You've saved my life already," he said, reaching into a bag. "See? I'm salivating."

"Here. Start chopping these vegetables for a salad."

"I don't have a knife."

Trish pulled a smaller sack out of the bag and unveiled a new knife. "Be prepared, I always say. I brought my own."

"Wow." Michael took the knife from her. "You think of everything."

"Not quite." A dark shadow passed across her eyes. "But at least we'll get this dinner together."

With Michael helping, the spaghetti sauce was soon bubbling in an old pot on the stove and the salad greens were tossed and put into a chipped ceramic bowl which had been left in the apartment. They ate off paper plates, laughing and joking, Michael assuring her at every turn that this was the best spaghetti he'd ever eaten.

When dinner was over, they sat cross-legged on the living room floor, eating the ice cream Trish had brought.

"I can't let you keep supporting me," Michael said, stretching out on his back. "You've got to move in and then it'll be okay."

Trish laughed "Ah-ha! I knew it! You picked me for my money."

"*You* picked *me*." He gave her a long look. "Will you move out, Trish?"

She placed her spoon on her paper plate and deliberately set it on the floor, taking her time. "I'd like to. I've sort of mentioned how I feel to my mom and stepfather."

"And?"

"I don't know." She made a face. "They say I'm too young. But I'm going to be eighteen in just a couple of months. I've even got a job lined up after school at Bo Peep's, that children's store downtown."

"Then do it. Get outta that war zone and come live with me."

"How'd you know it was a war zone?" she asked curiously.

"It's written all over you. Every time you bring up your family you get serious. Like tonight, when I said you think of everything. All of a sudden you looked different—like you just got hit with a bad memory. You were thinking about your stepfather, weren't you?"

Trish's lips parted in dismay. "No!"

"What is it, Trish? Did something happen you couldn't handle?"

"What do you mean?" She was on her feet, hurriedly brushing off her jeans.

"Hey, don't go." Michael got up, too, mad at himself for somehow scaring her away. "I'm sorry. Look, if you don't want to talk about it, forget it. It's history."

She shook her head. "It's late. I have to go anyway."

"Don't be mad."

"I'm not mad. Are you crazy?" She managed a weak smile. "You're the best friend I've got, Michael. I know that sounds stupid, since we've just met, but it's true."

"Then come back tomorrow. You don't even have to bring dinner."

"Michael . . ." She bit into her lower lip.

"Okay, the next night. I'm not pushy." At her continued silence, he said, "All right. You win. I'll give you 'til the end of the week, but then you've got to come over and save me from my own company."

This time her smile was more natural. "Are you really serious about my moving in with you? I mean really, really, serious?"

"Of course I am."

She nodded as she twisted open the door. "I'll—I'll try to work something out." Swallowing, she darted a look back in his direction. "I hate my stepfather. And I don't like my mom very much right now, either."

"Hey, I feel the same way."

"Good night," she said, and the door shut behind her.

"Good night," he answered to the empty room, but inside he was filled with new hope. Trish was going to be his roommate! At least she was going to try to be. And that, Michael decided, was nine-tenths of the battle.

Amanda was parked in the shadows across from Neil's house. A shawl covered her blond hair and she kept looking over her shoulder, certain someone was watching her. But it was only her frazzled nerves working on overload. There was nothing, and no one, to fear. Charles was still in the hospital and the only other person who understood how she felt was Neil himself.

Headlights came around the corner and Amanda averted her face. The car pulled into Neil's driveway and in relief, she realized he was finally home.

She got out of her car and quickly crossed the street. "Neil," she called softly.

"Amanda?" Neil appeared out of the dark gloom of his garage. "What are you doing here?"

"I had to see you. Oh, Neil. I'm such a wreck. Charles is just the same and I can't stand it."

"Shhh." He tucked her arm through his and led her around to the side door. "Didn't I tell you there's nothing to worry about?"

"But if someone finds out about us and tells Charles, it'll kill him!"

"Now don't go all melodramatic on me. Come here." In the security of his kitchen, away from prying eyes, Neil gave Amanda a long, lingering kiss. She smelled and tasted so good, and with his life crumbling around him, she was the one solid thing he could call his own. Yet, she wasn't his own, strictly speaking. She was still married to Charles Howard, and though in the beginning Neil had been glad that they couldn't get more involved, now he wasn't certain what he wanted.

She clung to him like a burr, her body trembling. "I'm not good at having an affair. It makes me feel terrible."

"When Charles is better you can get a divorce."

"What if he doesn't get better? What if he's this way for years and years? I couldn't take that!"

"We'll work something out."

"When? Neil, I've got to know!"

It was all he could do not to show his exasperation. As much as he cared about Amanda, her phobias sometimes got him down. And he had other problems, bigger problems, to occupy his time. Just thinking about them made him break into a cold sweat and he quickly went to fix himself and Amanda both a drink.

"Relax, Amanda. Charles's condition is improving, slowly. I checked on him at the hospital. They say he may come home in a couple of days."

She sat down next to him on the couch, gingerly, her hands twisting the stem of her wineglass around and around. Neil kissed her lightly on the cheek, realizing how much he needed her. Lately he'd felt like only half a man. His clientele had been slowly and steadily decreasing, and though he knew it was because he hadn't devoted enough time to being a doctor, he couldn't seem to change.

With an effort he shut off that particular line of thinking. Dr. Neil Curtis was a man who was used to being in charge. He refused to admit even to himself that gambling had him by the throat.

Setting down his drink, he carefully took Amanda's from her agitated fingers. Then he drew her into his arms, kissing her cheek and neck, indulging himself in the only luxury that really let him forget his troubles.

"I can't, Neil," Amanda said, gently extricating herself. "Not tonight. I'm too upset." She got up, gathered her coat and gloves, then gave him a sad, mournful look. "You understand, don't you?"

"Sure." Neil wiped a hand over his mouth. It was a lie. He didn't understand. All he knew was this godawful feeling of impending doom.

"I'll call you tomorrow," she said, then the back door clicked shut behind her.

Swirling the rest of the wine in his glass, Neil stared down at the ruby red liquid for a long, long time. Then he picked up the phone.

"Hi, Andy? It's Neil. Get me into that poker game Saturday night, okay? Yeah, I know it's high stakes, but don't worry. I'm prepared. I paid Jimmy and his boys off last week . . ."

As he spun the lie he felt as if Jimmy Sentra, the loan shark himself, was breathing down his neck. Involuntarily he glanced over his shoulder, a shiver sliding up his back.

If he could only score big on Saturday, then all his problems would be over!

* * *

Soft music was playing at Doug's Place as the band filled in with some slow love songs while the singer took a break. Tom and Alice Horton, Bill's parents, looked across the table at their son and daughter-in-law.

"What's the matter?" Tom asked, setting down his menu. "You two have hardly said three words since we got here."

"Nothing's wrong." Bill frowned down at his drink, ignoring the silent appeal he could feel emanating from his wife.

"Now that's a big, fat lie if I ever heard one, son."

Bill was silent and Laura attempted to fill the uncomfortable gap. "We've just had some problems with Michael, that's all."

Alice made a sound of commiseration. "Serious problems?"

"Serious enough," Laura admitted.

"Oh, what's the use in covering up." Bill exhaled a frustrated breath. "Michael's run away from home."

"Run away!" Alice's hand flew to her lips.

"Yes. Over a week ago."

"Have you called the police?" Tom asked.

"Not yet. We just—figured he would come home."

"I'm worried sick," Laura admitted, now that the truth was out. "What if something's happened to him? We've waited too long. Michael would have come back by now."

The corners of Bill's mouth turned down in bitterness. "I'm not so sure. He hates me. And he thinks Mickey's let him down. I think he's out there, and he just wants us to suffer."

"That's a pretty harsh statement, son." Tom's brows lifted.

"Well, I'm tired of all the garbage. We've all been afraid to tell Michael the truth. Why? Because he might do something drastic. Well, this is drastic," he said, pressing his index finger onto the table. "Now he's run away and God knows where he is. A lot of good it did not telling him I'm his father."

Alice looked from her son to Laura. "What do you plan to do?"

Laura shook her head, unable to speak for the tears welling in her throat. She drew a heavy breath, expelled it, then said, "As a mother, I want to call the police. I need to know where he is. But as a psychiatrist, I think he needs some space. He's almost eighteen and he's had tremendous emotional pressures." She shrugged unhappily. "I'm in this terrible limbo, not knowing what's right."

There was silence at the table. They gave their orders and soon hot and tempting dishes were set in front of each of them. But no one had any appetite.

Finally Bill said, "I think we'll wait until the first of next week. If he hasn't contacted us by then, we'll file a missing persons report."

The decision reached, the subject was closed. But no one at the table even attempted to pretend they were having a good time. They were all consumed by one collective worry: where was Michael?

"Would'ya look at that?" Brooke whispered, her eyes gleaming.

David stared up the winding driveway to the

imposing Tudor house capping the knoll. Lights shone from the paned windows like warm, yellow beacons. Against the overcast skies the place looked homey and inviting—and staggeringly expensive.

"She's done all right for herself, hasn't she?" Brooke commented.

"She always lands on her feet."

"No love lost between you and good old Mom, huh?"

David's expression was grim. "You could say that. Ready?"

"Oh, yeah." She settled back in her seat.

The old Ford protested with a backfire like the report from a gun and a stream of black smoke. David babied the car up the drive, noticing how immaculate the grounds were. Not a leaf dared to drift onto the driveway, though the maples had turned gold and orange.

His butterflies took flight again as he stopped in front of the brick porch. His hands were clammy. Switching off the ignition, he said, "Stay here until after I see if she's home."

"Oh, David."

"Just do it. I gotta see her by myself."

He followed the herringbone brick path to the porch, swallowing several times. It wouldn't do to let her see how he felt. It would ruin everything. He had to be cool. Cool and collected. There was no other way.

Pressing the doorbell, he ran his other hand nervously through his rain-darkened hair. His toe tapped a rapid beat against the bricks.

A light came on, shining down on him, and David held his breath. Then the door slowly opened.

Julie stood just inside the threshold.

"Hello . . . Mother."

His attempt at nonchalance fell short when his voice cracked, but David couldn't help himself. His throat was dry. His heart was pounding so hard he was sure it would choke him.

Her face paled and her lips parted. "David?" Julie whispered tremulously, disbelief in her voice.

"Yeah. I've come back. For a while."

"Oh, David!"

Before he could react she rushed out and threw her arms around him, weeping softly, hugging him with shaking arms. She said his name over and over again and he was powerless to do anything but stand stock-still in amazement. Inside, he had the strangest desire to cry, and it took all his willpower to fight back his emotions.

When she finally drew back her blue eyes were drenched with tears. But her lips were curved in a smile. "You don't know how glad I am to see you," she said brokenly. "Oh, David. You just don't know."

It was in his mind to tell her right then why he'd come. *You don't buy this maternal guilt trip, do you?* he reminded himself. But he couldn't get his tongue to form the words. Instead he just stared back, a sick smile plastered to his lips.

"Why don't you introduce us?" a voice said from behind his head.

He twisted on his heel. There stood Brooke, her back against one of the square brick posts supporting the porch, her arms folded over her chest. Her hair was a tangled mess, blowing across her eyes, but her gaze was determined and imperious.

"Uh, Mother . . . this is Brooke Hamilton."

"Hello, Brooke." Julie stepped forward eagerly.

In profile, through the shirt she had tucked into her slacks, David could discern a slight swelling in his mother's abdomen. Was she *pregnant?*

"Hello, Mrs. Anderson." Brooke was glacial. Belatedly David recognized the symptoms: she was jealous of his mother! "I'm David's fiancée."

David stared at her as if she'd lost her mind, but Julie took it in her stride. "I'm so glad to meet you." She turned back to David, eyes shining. "And I'm speechless when it comes to how I feel about having you back. Welcome home, David. Please, don't ever leave me again."

And with that introduction, Julie insisted they both come inside. Raising her brows as she passed David, Brooke followed after her. Chandeliers sparkled in the foyer. The patina of polished wood shone from the floor and was matched in the curved rail of the stair. An arrangement of full-blossomed fall flowers stood in a brass bowl on a sideboard.

Brooke smiled inwardly. This was even better than she'd imagined.

Chapter Three

Sweet Torture

The room was lit by candlelight; the chandelier had been dimmed to a soft, burnished glow. Crystal and silver gleamed. White china plates reflected their smooth luster.

David tried, not very successfully, to hide his awe. His mother had pulled out all the stops; nothing was too good for her son. The dinner had been prepared by caterers from one of Salem's most renowned firms, and in his jeans and faded shirt David felt like a poor, unwelcome relative. Except he wasn't unwelcome. For all the pomp and circumstance the conversation was light and friendly. Julie made no effort to hide how pleased she was to have him back.

"I'm so glad you're here," she said again, her face glowing with happiness. "Bob and I both are."

David looked to the head of the table, where his mother's husband was carving a prime rib roast. Each time Bob sliced across the meat, juices poured from the succulent beef. Now he lifted his silvered head and acknowledged Julie's statement. "Yes, it's a pleasure having you."

David couldn't figure out the relationship between his mother and Bob. On the surface it looked as if they had everything: money, prestige, respect for each other. Yet he felt undercurrents he didn't quite understand. Uneasily, his mind flew back to Doug Williams and his mother's infatuation with the man. Surely that was long over. She wouldn't have married Bob unless she truly loved him, would she?

"When's the baby due?" Brooke asked, as one of the caterers silently set a heaping plate in front of her.

"In the spring." Julie glanced toward Bob, then looked away.

"What are you hoping for, a boy or a girl?"

"A boy," Bob said, the first time he'd really spoken on his own. "I already have a daughter from my first marriage. Her name's Mary. This time around I want a son."

"What about you?" David asked his mother.

"Oh, I guess I'd like a girl," she said softly. "After all, I've got you."

It was all he could do to keep from squirming in his seat. This homecoming wasn't going like he'd planned at all. His mother was dragging him deeper and deeper into a quagmire of guilt. Did she know what she was doing? Or could this doting mother stuff be for real?

"Well, I'm with you Bob," Brooke said. "I want a boy. And I want him to look just like David."

An uncomfortable silence filled the room. "Are you planning a family right away?" Julie asked, frowning as she cut into her prime rib.

"Well, we haven't really talked about it." Brooke slid a smile to David.

It was suddenly more than he could take. "We haven't even set a date to get married yet," he said grimly. For reasons he was afraid to analyze too closely, it was imperative his mother know the truth.

"But you're back in Salem to stay?"

Julie's question was meant to be casual, but David could hear how much she yearned for him to say yes. He opened his mouth to answer, but Brooke intervened.

"We're just passing through," she said quickly. "David just wanted to—see you again." Under the table she gave him a kick, but all it served to do was make him angry.

"I'd like to stay around awhile, though," he admitted, ignoring the daggers shooting from Brooke's eyes. "It's been a long time."

"Yes, it has." Julie's tone was wistful, touched with the kind of remorse David wasn't ready to acknowledge.

Bob picked up his wineglass and looked directly at David. "Where are you planning on staying while you're here?"

"I don't know. We haven't figured that out yet."

"Oh, stay here!" Julie burst out. "There are lots of rooms."

The tension between Bob and Julie became almost palpable. Brooke felt it, too, and she glanced from one to the other of them, her eyes alight with interest.

"I wouldn't want to intrude—" David began, but Bob cut him off.

"Of course you'll stay here. Like your mother pointed out, there are lots of rooms."

After that the conversation slowly deteriorated

and by the time dinner was over, David was eager to go for a walk outside to clear his head. He knew Bob didn't want him there. But Julie did. And if he were ever going to get his inheritance out of her he was going to have to play it her way.

Brooke caught him at the French doors, trying to sneak outside. "Well, where are you going?" she demanded.

"Just for a walk. I need some fresh air."

"I'll come with you."

He would have preferred to be alone, but he knew Brooke wouldn't understand. They walked outside together, and she linked her arm through his.

"I can't wait to get out of here," she confided. "I mean, it's all nice and wonderful. They've got a lot of bucks. But your mother's just too creepy."

"What do you mean?" David stopped.

"The way she'd like to hang on to you. She even wants you to stay in this house! Her husband sure doesn't feel that way. I bet he wishes you and I would just disappear."

David stared up at the moon. He almost felt that way himself. "I think we will have to stay here, though—at least until I win back my mother's trust."

"You're not serious." Brooke was appalled.

"It's what she wants, and if I'm going to talk her into giving me my inheritance early, I'd better be the perfect son, don't you think?"

"I won't stay here!" She stalked away from him, infuriated. "I won't."

"Sweetheart, there's no other way."

Brooke clenched her teeth. There was always

another way. She hadn't grown up in a two-bedroom shack with an alcoholic mother who couldn't even support her without learning how to get what she needed by other means. It burned her that David was knuckling under to his mother. Instinctively, she recognized the woman as her enemy and she was going to do her damnedest to fight her.

"Brooke . . . ?"

She stiffened her back, refusing to look over her shoulder. But even in her anger she loved David. He was all she had. Her mother was nothing, a useless shell of a woman who had let one bad thing after another happen to Brooke. Only David cared about her, really cared.

His hand tentatively touched her shoulder. "Be mad if you want to, but this is the only thing to do."

"I don't like it." She slowly turned around. David was stubborn, but there were ways to change his mind. She let her hands slowly slide up the front of his shirt, her fingers delve in the tuft of hair curling over his open collar. "I don't like it at all."

"Neither do I. But you want me to get the money, don't you?"

"I want *you*, David. You haven't forgotten last night, have you? And the night before, and the night before that? We've been living together too long to suddenly sleep in separate rooms under your mother's roof." She rubbed her lips lightly against his. "And I have this feeling she won't let us stay together."

One of Brooke's main attractions was her sensual nature. It's what had drawn David to her in the beginning, before he'd discovered the unhappy woman beneath her tough exterior. The combination had triggered an instant response from him—like finding a kindred spirit. Now, as her fingers touched and tantalized, and her kisses grew increasingly seductive, he realized how much he'd come to depend on her, emotionally and physically. "It'll only be for a little while," he murmured, drawing her near. "I don't want to blow this chance."

"Neither do I. Can't we have it both ways? Let's go to a motel. Right now."

For a moment, while her spell worked its magic, David was torn. He didn't trust his mother, or anyone else. Anyone except Brooke. Then he heard the French doors open behind him.

"David?" It was Julie.

"Right here."

"Oh . . . I've got a pot of coffee brewing. Maybe we could sit down and talk for a while . . . if you'd like to . . ."

Later, he wondered what had possessed him, but at that moment he couldn't help but respond to Julie's tentative tone. Releasing Brooke, he walked back to the patio, closing his ears to her swift intake of breath. Too much was at stake for him to risk it all just to save her ego. "Brooke and I were just coming in," he called. Then, taking the plunge, he added, "We've decided we'd like to stay here with you."

"Wonderful! Come on in. I'll show you your rooms."

Life had a way of slamming you down, only to pick you up again, Michael decided, as he twisted the lug nuts off a tire. Lou had rejected his idea to open longer hours but now Michael could see him stewing over the idea. He wasn't surprised, therefore, when a few moments later, the crotchety fellow came over and grunted his approval. Longer hours, more pay. And if Trish would move in everything would be perfect. Except that he wasn't going to finish high school unless he figured something out fast.

The silver Lincoln cruised in right at closing time. With a wave, Michael ignored Lou's scowl and hurried to meet her.

"Hi," he said, getting in.

"Hi." Trish didn't smile.

"Something wrong?"

"I told my mom I was moving out."

Michael let out a low whistle. "And?"

"And she said okay."

"Well, that's great!" At her lack of jubilation, he asked, "Isn't it?"

"I don't know. I guess so. Could you—would you come home with me? She wants to meet you. Make certain you're on the level, if you know what I mean."

Michael snorted. "Make certain I'm not after your body, you mean."

"Yeah, right."

"What about your stepfather?"

Trish turned the Lincoln out of the gas station and headed on the main road, which wound around the riverfront and took them farther out of town. "What about him?"

"What did he say about your moving out?"

She bit into her lower lip. "He doesn't know yet."

"Oh."

Michael could easily read between the lines

and he realized there was more to this meeting with Trish's parents than she'd initially let on. It didn't bother him, however. He would be more than glad to meet a whole army of relatives if it ensured Trish's move to his apartment.

The Clayton house was modest but neatly kept up. In the driveway stood a black Triumph Spitfire—her stepfather's car, Trish informed him.

"Any last-minute advice before I venture into the war zone?" Michael whispered in her ear as they approached the front door.

"Keep cool. And let them know you have a girlfriend you're just wild about."

A girlfriend? The only girl he even knew was Trish and his feelings for her were ones he was interested in keeping to himself. But he said, "Well, that won't be a lie," just for the hell of it, to see how she would react.

Trish gave him a strange look, but then they were at the front door. She opened it and yelled, "Yoo-hoo! I'm home. I brought Michael with me. The friend I've been telling you about."

At first Michael thought the living room was empty, but then he saw a woman curled in the far chair by the window. The evening shadows had darkened the room but she hadn't bothered turning on a light. As Trish switched on the nearest lamp, the woman slowly rose. She had a faded loveliness that was echoed in her daughter, but there were tired lines of disillusionment around her mouth and when she looked at Michael no emotion lit her eyes.

"Mom, this is Michael Horton. He's the boy I'm going to share the apartment with."

Michael wondered if Trish's mother heard the

challenging note in her daughter's tone that he did.

"Hello," was all she said.

"Trish?"

A deep masculine voice sounded from the back of the house and Michael saw both Trish and her mother stiffen. Then a tall man came around the corner, pulling his suspenders back over the shoulders of his T-shirt as he walked in the room. There was something about the way he smiled at Trish that gave Michael the creeps.

Unconsciously, Trish sidled closer to Michael. "This is my stepfather," she said in a low voice. "Jack Clayton."

The man stuck out a beefy hand to Michael. "That's right. And who are you, boy?"

"Michael Horton."

"You Trish's young stud?" he asked, then laughed uproariously, looking at his wife for support. The woman just turned away, staring out the window.

"Trish is a friend of mine," Michael said, gritting his teeth together. *Man, oh man, is this guy a loser!* "I have a girlfriend in Salem."

"Is that right?" He walked over to Trish, wrapped an arm around her shoulders, and gave her a huge squeeze. For a moment Trish looked panicked and Michael took a step closer, but Jack let her go. "Well, I'm glad to hear it, boy, 'cause Trish is my baby. I love her like my own child. Wouldn't want anybody hurtin' her. You understand what I'm saying?"

"I think so."

"Now I don't really want her leaving home. Jeri's told me what her plans are, but I can't go along with them."

"You don't have a choice." Trish, a bit paler, was nevertheless making a stand. Without looking directly into Jack Clayton's eyes, she added firmly, "I'm moving my stuff out tonight. I already told Mom. She said it's okay."

"Jeri's not the man of this household, little lady," Jack warned with a shake of his head.

"She's my mother. Please don't make an issue of this, Jack. Please. I—I really want to be out on my own."

The most amazing aspect of all, Michael thought, was that Jeri Clayton acted as if she weren't even involved. She just kept staring out the window, brooding, totally withdrawn.

Jack ran a hand over his jaw. His gaze narrowed on his wife for several moments, then he turned back to Trish. "Looks like you've already made up your mind."

Trish didn't answer.

"Well, if this is really what my little girl wants, maybe we could give it a try." He skewered a look at Michael. "You'd better mean it about this other girlfriend or you'll have me to answer to. On the other hand, I like the idea of Trish having a man around to protect her. You understand?"

"Yes."

Trish couldn't hide her jubilation. It was as if she'd been holding her breath, because now it came out in a huge sigh of relief. "I'll get some things right now. Enough for tonight. I'll pick up the rest tomorrow."

While Trish ran to pack, Michael waited uncomfortably in the Clayton living room. Jeri Clayton continued to be uncommunicative, and Jack Clayton just put Michael's teeth on edge.

Trying not to display his nervousness, Michael counted the minutes until Trish returned.

"You can take the Lincoln," Jeri said, breaking her silence when Trish finally reappeared. "Bring it back tomorrow."

"Thanks, Mom." Trish gave her a quick peck on the cheek.

She would have left then, her hand was already on the door, when Jack said, "Whoa there! What about one for your old man?"

You could have heard a pin drop as Trish slowly turned around. Michael's heart bled for her as she reluctantly walked back to her stepfather. She was on tiptoes, intending to give him the same quick kiss she gave her mother, when Jack suddenly scooped her near, planting a huge kiss right on her lips. Then he swatted her behind and said, "Be a good girl, now. See ya tomorrow."

They were outside before Trish reacted and then she bolted across the yard, throwing herself over the hood of the Lincoln, her chest heaving wildly. Michael walked at a slower rate and when he reached her she lifted her head, regarding him wordlessly for a long moment.

"I understand," was all he said, and Trish made a choking sound and threw her arms around his neck, shaking all over.

"Hello, Mom?" Brooke chewed on a fingernail, praying she would find her mother sober enough to talk this time. As useless an endeavor as it probably was, she hoped her mother was currently bucks up enough to send her some money. Though Julie Anderson was more than willing to give David all the money he needed,

David, for God knew what reason, refused to take it.

"I'm just holding out for my inheritance," he'd assured Brooke earlier that morning. "I don't want to seem like a leech."

She'd argued long and hard with him but to no avail. Waiting for his inheritance was all fine and good if you had enough money to keep going. Unfortunately, Brooke didn't.

"Brookie?" Adele's voice was slurred and Brooke's hopes sank.

"Are you drunk?" she demanded. "Mom, I need money. I'm broke and I don't know what to do."

"Ahh, Brookie, come home. Your mama needs you."

In the background Brooke heard the sound of a bottle crash to the floor. Infuriated beyond all reason, she swore and slammed down the receiver.

She couldn't depend on anyone these days!

"I'd be happy to sleep on the couch," Trish argued. "It's your apartment, Michael. You take the bedroom."

"You call that a couch? Not even close. It takes a master to figure out how to sleep on the thing without being speared by the springs. You take the bed."

Trish had had the foresight to bring a sleeping bag, several blankets, and a pillow. She argued valiantly for equal rights but in the end ended up with the bed and blankets while Michael won the sleeping bag and pillow. He lay in the dark, his hands behind his head, and listened to her go through the motions of getting

ready for bed. The window was cracked and a
cool breeze blew across his face, cooling the
thoughts that seemed to have arisen out of
nowhere. A girlfriend. Trish was the only
girlfriend he wanted.

Groaning a little, he buried his face in the pillow. Emotions he hadn't wanted to acknowledge
flooded through him like a molten river. He lay
in silent agony until he couldn't stand it any
longer. Then quietly he got up and dressed and
let himself out the front door.

He walked for what felt like hours and in the
end came to stand by the phone booth near
Lou's Garage. Before he really thought through
what he was doing, he'd dialed his mother's
house.

"Hello?" Laura's voice was foggy with sleep.

"Mom? It's Michael."

Her breath drew in sharply. "Michael! Oh,
Michael." She started to cry.

"Look, Mom, I'm okay," he said hurriedly,
pulling up the collar of his coat. He felt like a
heel. "Everything's fine. I just didn't want you to
worry anymore."

"When are you coming home?" She could
hardly talk through her tears.

He pinched the bridge of his nose. Why had
he called? Why had he felt this urgency to
touch base with home? He couldn't go back—
not the way things stood. "Ahh, I'm not coming
home," he said.

"Well, where are you?" She was baffled,
upset.

"I'm not that far away. I'll call you back
later." He was in the act of hanging up when
her pleading voice arrested him.

"Michael, please! Please don't go. Talk to me. If—if you don't want to come home, I'll try to understand. But don't hang up. Please . . ."

His chest hurt. Swallowing against a dry throat, he said, "I'm working, Mom. I've got a job. And I want to get back into school and graduate."

"You haven't missed that much," said Laura eagerly. "You always got good grades and the teachers at South Salem High—"

"No. I'm going to finish school here. I want to be on my own."

"Where, exactly, is here?"

"I'll call you back. Good-bye."

Heart pounding, Michael pressed his finger against the receiver. Suddenly he'd felt the walls closing in on him. He'd remembered how Bill had treated him, how his mother had looked at him, her eyes sad and soulful. He couldn't take it again. His new life was too important to him.

So why the phone call? he asked himself as he began the long walk back to the apartment.

With an inward grimace he realized seeing Trish's parents had upset him. Guilt had prompted the call to his mother. And if he reached down deep inside, he knew that his platonic relationship with Trish hadn't been giving him the emotional support he needed. He'd needed something more.

Kicking a can out of the street, he swore under his breath. As glad as he was that she'd moved in, it was going to be a hellish kind of sweet torture. She'd gotten under his skin.

The whir from the hospital bed brought Amanda running down the hall, but Charles was just adjusting the back. He gave her a smile, looking better than she'd seen him in weeks. His pallor was still gray, however, but the doctors had assured her that would disappear with time.

"He's getting better every minute," they'd said several days earlier. "We're releasing him Tuesday."

And now here he was, back home. Even the hospital bed hadn't been truly necessary but Amanda had insisted upon it. She was a nervous wreck. The responsibility of Charles's health weighed upon her like a load of bricks.

Seeing her anxious face, Charles said, "Relax, my love. I'm fit and chipper. I won't be an invalid for long."

"Do you need anything? Something to eat or drink?"

"No, don't baby me. Just go ahead and do whatever it is you usually do."

Amanda's conscience nagged her. She'd been spending every spare evening with Neil. "I'll go downstairs and read," she murmured. "Unless you want me to stay."

"No. Go on." He waved her away.

She gave him an uncertain look, then disappeared down the hall. As soon as she was out of sight Charles ground his teeth together, his hand stealing to his chest. Yes, he was better. He could feel it. But he couldn't stand the slow pace of his recovery.

"Amanda!"

She was in his room like a shot and it annoyed him, made him feel his age. Knowing the only way to do what he wanted was to get rid of her, he said, "Why don't you go to a movie or something? I'm going to sleep and I don't want to think about you sitting here all alone."

"I couldn't leave you, Charles."

"I insist. I can get up and walk anywhere I need to. Go on. It would make me happy."

"I don't know . . ." she said dubiously.

"Go visit a friend. It'll put my mind at ease to know you're out having fun."

Wincing inside, Amanda finally said, "There's a double feature at the Southside Cinema I've been wanting to see."

"Perfect." Charles yawned. "I just want to rest."

It was wrong, she told herself a few minutes later, as she searched through her purse for her keys. She shouldn't leave him yet. But in all truthfulness, her relief at getting out of the house was enormous.

She drove toward the Southside Cinema, fully intending to see the double feature, when somehow she found herself turning onto the quiet, tree-lined streets near Neil Curtis's house.

This isn't like you, she thought. *You wouldn't do this to Charles.*

Yet, here she was, parking in her usual place across the street. Amanda sighed, locking her car. She had to face the awful truth about herself once and for all. She loved Neil. Charles was just a millstone around her neck.

She could hear soft music playing from inside Neil's house. Rapping quickly on the door, she counted the seconds until Neil answered it.

"Amanda!" he said. "You came." Holding open the door, he pulled her inside. "My God, it feels like ages since I've seen you."

"Neil," she whispered, shaking. She wound her arms around his neck, kissing him fervently. He responded with the same kind of desperation.

They stood against the wall, holding on to each other with a passion that had been simmering between them for months. Charles's turn for the better had made them both realize how hard it was not to see each other whenever they wanted.

"Don't leave me, Amanda."

"No. Never."

"Let's go upstairs."

Neil dimmed the lights as they went. At the bedroom door, Amanda hesitated, and Neil gave her a searching look.

"Don't think about him," he said. "Think about us."

He began to undress her and Amanda shivered, as much from her own guilt as desire. But she couldn't leave, couldn't resist. She wanted to build her life around Neil out of the ashes of an unhappy past.

"Love me, Neil. Just love me," she whispered.

In the darkness, he took her into his arms. Amanda blocked out thoughts of Charles and lived for the moment. This was now. Neil was her future. They both sensed it might be their last intimate encounter for a long, long time.

The telephone shrilled, startling them both.

"It's Charles!" Amanda said fearfully.

"Shhh. It can't be. He doesn't know you're here."

"He found out! He found out! I know he did!"

He clapped his hand over her mouth, muffling her hysteria, as the telephone rang again, loud and sharp in the darkness. "Listen to me. It's not Charles. It's got to be for me. Now be quiet . . . please."

He slowly lifted his hand, feeling her heart

racing against his bare chest. But Amanda didn't speak. She lay trembling and afraid at his side.

"Dr. Curtis," he answered the phone.

"Well, Doctor, how are you doin'? I've been waitin' ta hear from you."

Jimmy Sentra's nasal tones struck a cold dagger in Neil's heart. It took him a moment to answer. "I was going to call you."

"When? Which century, Doctor?"

"As soon as I worked—everything out."

"The way I heard it," the loan shark went on, "you lost a bundle at Andy's poker game last Saturday night. How're you gonna pay me, huh, when you're droppin' money all over town?"

Neil rolled away from Amanda. This couldn't be happening. "Let me call you in the morning. It's not convenient for me to talk right now."

"Oh, sure. Sure. I'll be hangin' by the phone." The sarcasm fell away and steel entered his voice. "Call by nine, Doc. No later."

"Who was that?" Amanda whispered, when Neil slowly replaced the receiver.

"Uh, no one. Just a slight problem I have to work out."

Tugging the sheet to her neck, Amanda shivered. The romantic mood had evaporated with the first peal of the telephone. "I should go home."

Neil didn't answer; he was too lost in thought. Taking his silence as a sign he didn't want her to stay, Amanda quickly slipped out of bed and dressed. She felt terrible, forgotten, dirty.

Distractedly, Neil, too, pulled on his clothes. "I'm sorry," he said. "I've just got things on my mind."

Don't we both, Amanda thought bitterly.

He gave her a kiss good-bye at the door but his heart wasn't in it.

As always, as soon as she was away from him and back in the real world, she felt depressed. Hating herself, she drove through the dark, silent streets back home. Tears slipped down her cheeks.

The house was just as she'd left it. She went inside and locked the door behind her. In the kitchen, she nearly tripped over a small barbell, one Charles was going to use to build up his strength.

Funny, she didn't remember dropping it there. Pouring herself a glass of water, Amanda looked at the barbell, perplexed.

Suddenly the water glass slipped from her hand and broke on the tile floor. Heart in her throat, she ran upstairs to Charles's room. The light was on.

"Charles?"

He was lying face down on the floor.

"Oh, God!"

Amanda rushed to his side, carefully turning him over. Shaking fingers searched for a pulse, but found none.

Silent anguish rose in her throat. He was dead. *Dead*. The room blurred in front of her eyes and the walls reverberated with the sound of her screams.

Chapter Four
A Secret Unveiled

Susan Peters stared at her husband is disbelief. "You're going to work *now*?" she questioned, stopping in mid-stride. The individual glass bowls of caramel flan were suspended in her hands.

Greg gently took his dessert from her unresisting fingers. "Not until after I've finished dinner."

"At this time of night?" Quick as a cat Susan swept the bowl away from him, sending it crashing against the far wall.

"What the hell—" Greg roared.

"I spend all day making you a special dinner and this is how you treat me! Just what are you doing at work these days?"

"I'm busy." Greg's face was red, his teeth clenched. He slammed back his chair and reached for his coat in one fluid motion.

"Busy doing what? Whose blood pressure are you taking at ten o'clock at night?"

Greg's temper rose like the quicksilver mercury in a thermometer. He jerked open the front door, but Susan grabbed him by the arm. They had a short, furious struggle and then he broke free of her grasp. "In case you're interested," he said through his teeth, "Neil's been slacking off and I'm trying to limp through our patients alone."

"Really. What sex are those patients? Female?"

The door slammed shut so violently the windows rattled in their casings. Susan yanked on the handle, swearing wildly. When she got it open Greg was already in his car.

"Damn you!" she screamed against the howling autumn wind.

The engine roared to life and he was gone in a squeal of tires.

Neil searched through the paper until he found the obituaries. There it was: Charles Howard. The man had died because he'd strained his heart, exercising too strenuously. He shook his head, disbelieving, and wondered how Amanda was faring. He hadn't seen her since the night Charles had died.

Looking around the kitchen, Neil ran a hand over his stubbled face and grimaced. What a disaster. Breakfast dishes still in the sink, papers scattered, coffee pooled on the counter. He needed a maid, that's what.

And how are you going to afford one?

Flinging the paper aside, he did a quick mental tally of his assets. He'd had to give Jimmy Sentra what was left of his savings with the promise of more by the first of the month. But even with his hefty salary, he knew he'd never be able to meet the commitment.

It didn't help that Greg Peters had been complaining about picking up the slack. What an ingrate. Neil had helped set him up, had made him a partner, and all Peters could do was nag about his hours.

Feeling restless, Neil checked the time and thought about calling Amanda. But he stopped himself. It wouldn't do to see her so soon after the funeral; it was almost worse now than before. Then, he would have been able to pass her off as a patient, like he had with Greg Peters, but now, well, she was a wealthy, young widow and that made her a prime candidate for gossip.

He would just have to wait.

With a sigh, he cleaned up the worst of the mess and headed for his office, wondering how many bills he could neglect and make it seem he'd just been forgetful before Greg caught on.

"You didn't expect to like me, did you?" Julie said, twirling a daisy between her fingers as they walked along the garden path.

David was at a loss for words.

A sad smile of wisdom touched the corners of her mouth. "Oh, I know what you thought of me, really. Spoiled, selfish, a first-class pain in the butt."

"Mom . . ." David protested weakly.

"Do you realize that's the first time you've even called me 'Mom'? Oh, David, don't look like that. Maybe I have been spoiled and selfish. But I've never stopped loving you."

They were at the end of the path, near the gazebo. The skies were overcast, but a weak sun made summer seem like more than a memory. David stopped by the bottom step, worrying a nail out of a board with the toe of his boot.

He didn't like it when his mother said things like that. It made him feel strange and unhappy. And the way she looked at him, with those beautiful blue eyes—eyes that seemed shadowed by a secret sadness—made him hurt way down deep.

"I know why you came back," she said.

David's heart flip-flopped. She knew?

"You wanted to see me again—" she shrugged "—maybe even to get back at me a little. That's why Brooke looks at me the way she does."

"Like how?" He breathed easier.

"Like I'm poisonous. Terrible." Julie squinted and glanced back down the path. "Here she comes now."

David followed her gaze. Brooke was indeed coming down the path at a pace that left no question about her frame of mind. She was furious. Even from a distance he could see the way her jaw was set.

"I'm sorry about Brooke," he heard himself say, then was horrified at the admission. But Julie just grinned, standing on her tiptoes to give him a quick kiss on the cheek.

"It's all right. Well, hello, Brooke," she greeted affably.

"Hello, Julie." In a gesture rife with double meaning, she slid her arm through David's, her gaze a steady challenge.

Conversation was stilted and tense and after a few moments Julie headed back to the house. With conflicting emotions David watched her leave, realizing how subtly she'd changed his plans. Now he didn't want his inheritance. Now he didn't want to go.

"What was she saying to you?" Brooke frowned at David's expression.

"Nothing much."

"How long are we going to have to stay here? I can't take much more of this."

"Oh, grow up, Brooke," he said in disgust and turned on his heel.

Stunned by his rejection, she gaped at him. But her survival instincts, never too far out of reach, surged to her rescue. "Grow up? Look who's talking. Your mother just crooks her finger and you come running."

"Give it a rest," he growled, walking away fast.

Brooke ran after him. "What's the matter, David? Am I hitting too close to the bone?"

"You're just making a bad situation worse."

"Oh, am I? Well, you've been different ever since we got here. And don't tell me it's all an act to get your inheritance because I won't believe it. No, you like it here."

"And what's wrong with that?" David demanded, stopping dead to glare at her. "What's wrong with wanting to come back?"

"I knew it! Sweet, perfect Mommy's got her little boy right where she wants him."

Brooke's taunting was the last straw. David grabbed her by the shoulders, wanting to shake her, wanting to make her see what he only half-understood himself.

But her eyes suddenly filled with tears, confusing him further. "I'm leaving, David," she said. "Right now. You can come with me if you want, but I'm hightailing it out of here."

"Brooke . . ."

He attempted to pull her close but she

wrenched away. Her tears were more from anger than distress, but she let them flow freely, hoping David would run after her.

On the porch she knew she'd miscalculated. David had chosen his mother. Resentment filled her and she squeezed her eyes shut, wishing some dire misfortune would hit Julie and strike her down.

"Are you all right?"

Startled, Brooke's lids flew open. It was Bob. He was standing on the porch, eyeing her with an expression that hovered somewhere between concern and mistrust.

"I'm fine."

"Are you sure?" His eyes delved into hers and Brooke noticed what an attractive man he was. At first all she'd thought was how much older he was than Julie, but there was more to Bob Anderson than she'd first guessed.

"Yes, I'm sure." She swiped the tears away. "But I'm leaving. Your wife—doesn't want me to stay."

"Julie?"

"She thinks I have too much influence on David."

"That's preposterous. You're his fiancée."

Brooke let her lower lip tremble. "Well . . . no . . . not exactly. Since we got here, David's called off the wedding. I don't know what to do."

"I'll handle this," he said grimly, and she had to stifle a smile. Let Julie wriggle her way out of this one.

"Are you coming in?" he asked, but she shook her head.

"I'm going back home," she said tearfully.

"But, Brooke . . ."

"It's no use. Do you—do you think you could take me to the bus station?"

"No, I mean yes, but I don't think—"

"Please, Bob." She laid a hand on his arm. "I don't want to cause any trouble. I want to leave, now." In her mind she had the whole scenario worked out. A few days away and David would realize how much he needed her.

"Well, if you're sure," Bob said dubiously.

"Oh, believe me, I'm sure."

Jeri Clayton dropped Trish off at the apartment she shared with Michael. She helped Trish unload more of her clothes and possessions, all the while keeping her thoughts to herself.

When the final item had been hauled inside, Trish pushed back her hair and said with a touch of belligerence, "Well?"

"Well, what?"

"Well, what do you think, Mom?"

"It's nice."

Trish sighed impatiently. "I mean about everything. The whole situation. Michael." She threw out her arms and twirled to encompass the whole apartment. "You haven't said boo about how you really feel."

Jeri Clayton had always been a private person, but over the last few months she'd suffered a personality change that had alarmed Trish. Now Jeri studied the small dimensions of the apartment and said, "This boy is just a friend, isn't he?"

"I told you he was. I wouldn't lie."

Jeri nodded. "Then I think this is the best situation for all of us."

Trish felt chilled. "Mom . . ."

Jeri turned, looking very old and very tired. "I'm not blind, Trish. If you need anything, call. Jack'll be glad to give you whatever you want."

Jeri left before Trish could demand an explanation of that cryptic remark, yet deep in her heart she was afraid she already knew the answer. Jack Clayton. Just thinking about him made goose bumps rise on her arm.

Why did everything have to be so complicated? she thought. *Thank God for Michael!*

With her confidence renewed, she hummed a tuneless song and began to put her things away, feeling oddly self-conscious as she moved Michael's clothes into the bathroom linen closet and made room for her own.

Amanda awakened with a start, her body drenched in sweat. "Charles?" she whispered.

But she was alone in the house. Charles was dead.

She lay quiet and still. Her mind played tricks on her. Was that the bottom step she heard squeak? There was a light shining beneath her bedroom door and she didn't remember leaving any on.

With all the courage she could muster, she dropped her legs over the side of the bed, her feet sinking into the cushy carpet. She walked to the door, her hand poised above the knob. But she couldn't open it! She was too afraid.

A glimpse of her nightmare returned. Charles, pointing a finger at her.

It's all your fault.

With a muffled cry Amanda beelined back to bed and under the covers, hands over her face. She would never get over her betrayal.

* * *

The dirt-encrusted bus bumped and rattled over potholes on the country road. Brooke looked out the window, her face set. Mentally she counted the money she had left. Twenty-three dollars and fourteen cents. Bob had been generous.

He hadn't wanted her to go at all, the poor old fool. For some reason her plight had made him go all paternal, and he'd sincerely wanted her to stay.

If only David had felt the same way.

Sighing, she determined she was not going to give up now. Oh, no. Not by a long shot. David was hers, and if he needed a little space to figure that out, okay. She'd go back to her mom for a few days and see if there was anything worth salvaging at home.

It was nightfall before the bus lumbered into Ash Grove. Brooke stepped onto the curb, stretched, then started the trek to the run-down post—World War II tract home she'd grown up in. A strong wind blew at her back, dewy with rain. She was glad to see a light on when she reached the rusted gate, gladder still to hear the black and white television blaring.

Adele must be home.

Brooke didn't bother knocking. She just pulled back the screen and pushed open the door.

To her disgust her mother was sprawled over the living room couch. The smell of stale alcohol was rank. With suppressed fury Brooke flung open a window.

"Mom, wake up!" she demanded, shaking Adele's shoulder.

"Brookie?"

"I didn't come all the way back here from Salem just to baby a drunk."

"Brookie . . ." Adele murmured again, dropping her elbow over her eyes as Brooke switched on the light.

This was a scene Brooke had played out over and over again during her childhood. She'd hardened her heart to it, knowing her mother would never change. But a deep, vulnerable part of her that refused to die cried out in agony anyway, and she had to go out to the weed-choked backyard and breathe deeply several times.

When she came back inside the light had been dimmed again, but Adele was half-sitting, her shoulder resting heavily on the arm of the couch. "S'at you, Brooke?" she asked.

"Who else would it be?"

"I—did you say you were—in Salem?"

"Mom, I need money. Have you got any? Ever since we went to Salem we've been staying with David's mom, but he won't ask for anything and she's rich. It's so unfair. I just can't stand it!"

"Salem . . ." Adele put a trembling hand to her forehead.

"Yeah, Salem." Brooke flung herself into the only other chair and plucked at the threadbare arms. "She's turning David's head and I hate it! She's got all this money and all he wants is his inheritance, but he thinks he has to play this game with her and it makes me sick."

"I lived in Salem, once."

Brooke threw her an impatient glance, snapping on another lamp. "I know you lived in Salem once. I know all about how beautiful you were when you were young and how all the men wanted you. But this is my life we're talking about. This is important, Mom. I'm telling you about Julie Anderson."

"Anderson?" Adele's voice changed.

"Yes, Anderson. Mrs. Bob Anderson."

Adele sat straight up, blinking against the glare from the unshaded bulb. "Bob Anderson of Anderson Construction?"

"You know him?" Brooke leaned forward. Though she'd heard her mother talk of the glory days often enough, she'd never given her much credence. Always her reminiscences were cloaked in romantic, fairy-tale trappings. Adele had even tried to make Brooke's father sound like a white knight, though she'd always suspected she'd been conceived from a one-night stand.

"Robert Anderson." Adele slowly shook her head, the haggard lines of her face softening. "I loved him, but he never knew about you. How funny that you found him all on your own."

Brooke stared blankly at her mother. "What do you mean?" she asked slowly.

"Can't you guess? He's your father, Brookie."

She was on her feet, her fists at her side, screaming before she even knew it. "Don't you lie to me!"

"I'm not lying," Adele said, blinking hard. "Bob Anderson's your father. I even put his name on your birth certificate."

"I don't believe you!"

"It's the truth. It was in the springtime after one of the hardest winters we'd ever seen. The snow had just begun to melt and the air was cool and sweet. I was only sixteen, y'know, and I—"

"Shut up!" Brooke ran out of the house, the screen banging shut behind her. Her chest heaved. Tears stood in her eyes.

It wasn't true. None of it was true. It was just more wild ramblings from a pathetic, broken woman who still lived in the past. She wouldn't believe it. She couldn't. Because if it were true, then her father was a monster who'd lived like a king while his daughter had been brought up in squalor.

She hadn't realized it before, but she preferred the white-knight theory. Better to have a father who might charge to your rescue at any time. And though the part of Brooke that dealt in reality knew she should be glad she finally had a father, the other part, the part that still believed in dreams, rejected the idea outright. Bob Anderson was not her father.

But then, how had Adele known about him?

The screen creaked open and Adele leaned against the doorjamb. "Come on in and fix me a drink, huh? We'll talk. Just like old times."

Her mouth turning down at the corners, Brooke accepted the bitter pill of truth. "You tell me everything," she said flatly. "Everything. But we're drinking coffee, Mom. No more booze."

It seemed as though the rain had let up just for today's trip, David thought, as he walked alongside his mother through the weekend outdoor market. The vendors displayed brightly painted stands with striped awnings, as if color alone could ward off the encroaching chill of winter.

"Here. You hold the sack and I'll pick out the apples," Julie said.

David watched as she selected different kinds.

"What are you gonna do with all these?" he asked, biting into a crisp red one.

"Stave off a total pig-out." She patted her softly rounded abdomen. "It's been a while since I had you. I'm afraid if I'm not careful I'll become a blimp."

"No way. You look great."

Julie glanced sideways at him, in time to see color sweep up his neck to his ears. "Thank you," she said lightly.

They walked on, still selecting fruit, but David's mind wandered. He saw himself as he'd been just a few short weeks before: resentful, angry, cynical, grasping. But he'd changed. He could practically feel the changes happening inside him.

He hoped he wasn't setting himself up for a fall.

They passed a flower vendor, a stooped woman, her face wreathed in wrinkles. On impulse, David bought a handful of daisies and presented them to Julie.

"You were twisting that one around the other day," he said awkwardly. "I just thought . . ."

"You thought right," Julie whispered tenderly. Unable to restrain herself any longer, she wrapped her arms around him and gave him a fierce hug. "Don't you ever leave me again. I couldn't stand it."

"I'll—try not to," David managed to get out. Guiltily, he thought of Brooke. Where was she? What was she doing? He still cared for her, but he knew instinctively that he was going to have to make a choice: Brooke or his mother.

He was afraid to consider who that choice might end up being.

• • •

Amanda stretched her arms out in front of her. Her hands shook uncontrollably. The nightmares were making her a wreck in the day as well as at night. If she envisioned Charles pointing at her one more time she would go mad; she was sure of it.

Knowing she needed help, she first considered Neil. She hadn't seen him since Charles's death; she'd been afraid to. But now she needed him more than ever and with that thought firmly in mind, she drove to the offices of Drs. Curtis and Peters.

"I'm sorry, Mrs. Howard. Dr. Curtis isn't in right now," Roxie, the receptionist, informed her. "Would you like to schedule an appointment?"

"No, thank you . . ."

"Roxie, could you get me the file on Carl Townsend?" a male voice interrupted. "I need to see it right away."

Amanda recognized Greg Peters's voice before he appeared in the doorway that led to the inner hall. Not wanting to be seen, she turned and headed for the door.

"Oh, hello. Did you want to see Dr. Curtis?"

It took her a moment to realize he was speaking to her. "Uh, yes, but he's not here."

Dr. Peters was young and athletic and his eyes held a friendly kind of empathy. He moved quickly, blocking her way to the door, confusing Amanda so that she stood helpless in the center of the room.

"Could I help?" he asked.

"No. I don't think so." She gauged the distance around him, wishing she wasn't such a teary mass of nerves. She didn't want Greg Peters or anyone else involved with her problems.

"I've been handling a lot of Neil's patients lately, Miss . . . ?"

"Howard." Her voice was a whisper, and she cleared her throat. "Amanda Howard. It's, er, Mrs. Howard. I'm a widow."

"Why don't you come in my office and we'll talk."

She wanted to refuse, but ended up lifting her shoulders in acquiescence more out of a lack of energy than a wish to confide. But once inside Greg's comfortable office with its tooled leather chairs and oak desk and credenza, she realized how quickly she could be seduced into telling all.

"I'm sorry, Dr. Peters. I can't—"

"Please, call me Greg."

"Greg," she said hesitantly. "I can't talk to you about my problems. They're personal."

He steepled his fingers on the desk. "Then you're not one of Neil's patients?"

"Not really." Amanda fidgeted with her coat, unconsciously causing the fabric to slide away, revealing one smooth, supple nyloned leg. In her agitation she barely noticed. But Greg did.

He didn't really understand the forces that drove him; he only knew that as soon as he'd seen her, looking so lost and forlorn in the reception room, he'd wanted to help her. She intrigued him. She represented something intangible he longed for, something he desired that was just out of reach. Lately Susan had become a nagging bore, ready to fly off the handle at the least little thing. He appreciated Amanda's helplessness, her vulnerability. There was a sweetness of character inside her that rivaled even her beauty.

"Thank you, Dr. Peters—Greg—but I've got to work this out with—Dr. Curtis." Amanda shook her head when he tried to protest, and before he could stop her she was gone.

Greg was left to stare thoughtfully at the place where she'd been. The faintest touch of perfume still lingered, hauntingly reminding him of her presence.

He shook his head and breathed deeply. What was the matter with him? He had a wife at home. Sure, they were having some tough times, but that was no reason to start dreaming about Amanda Howard. She was Neil's woman, or so she'd intimated.

For the rest of the afternoon Greg went about his business, fully intending to forget her. But it wasn't easy. Her image kept reappearing in his mind's eye—beautiful, tempting, so needful of a strong man.

Amanda Howard. What was it about her that was so irresistible?

Brooke stood at the edge of the imposing Anderson yard, just inside the gate. The initial shock of learning Bob was her father had worn off and now she accepted it as fact. But what good would it do her?

To Brooke's way of thinking, this new wrinkle didn't affect her situation with David. *He* was all that mattered. She just had to get him away from Julie and everything would be perfect. Finding out about Bob had thrown her off, but now, well, she would just bide her time on that.

But she had to get David back. Right away.

With that thought as her guide, Brooke walked up to the porch and rang the bell. They would have to take her back: David, Julie, and Bob, too.

If not she would blurt out the whole sordid truth.

Chapter Five
The Setup

"Why didn't you insist that he come home?" Bill worried aloud again. "Didn't he tell you anything about where he is?"

Laura eyed him over the rim of her coffee cup. For days she'd been harangued with the same questions, yet she could hardly blame Bill. He'd been horrified when her call with Michael had ended so abruptly.

"He said he'd call again. He will. Just give him time."

"Time? I've given him time! He's just a kid."

"A kid with adult problems. Please, Bill, I don't like it any better than you do but at least we know he's safe."

"Do we? We only know what he tells us."

Laura snapped the newspaper out in front of her. She didn't want to have a fight, not so early in the morning. "I've got to get to the office. I have a new patient coming in this afternoon and I want to be prepared."

"Oh?" He didn't even try to sound interested.

"Her name's Amanda Howard. We had one

meeting and she was extremely nervous. But she called again yesterday. I'm glad. I really think she needs help."

There was no answer this time so Laura lowered the newspaper, peeking over the top at her husband. Her heart went out to him. He looked so troubled and unhappy.

Placing her hand over his, she said, "Michael's got terrible growing pains, Bill. It'll be over soon. You wait and see. He'll be back before you know it."

"How can you be sure?"

"I'm not sure. I'm hopeful. He didn't sound bitter on the phone at all. It was more—wistful. Like he misses us but can't quite admit it yet."

Bill looked at his wife. Her face, so fresh and earnest, made some of his tension disappear. "What did I do to deserve you?"

"I'll have to give it some thought."

"That hard to remember, huh?"

She folded the paper and came around the table, motioning him to scoot back his chair. Then she sat down on his lap. "You've been a real pain," she admitted with a smile.

"Thanks."

"But I love you anyway." She kissed the crown of his head. "Now stop worrying. Michael's happy and he's determined to finish school. The rest will just take time."

He gave her a squeeze and sighed. "I suppose you're right again, Doctor."

"You suppose?"

"Okay, I know. Satisfied?"

"Not quite." She leaned down and gave him the kind of kiss that foreshadowed what he could expect later that evening.

* * *

Julie swept up her purse, trying hard not to let Brooke get under her skin. "Are you sure you won't come?" she asked again, her hand on the door.

There was a sullen insolence about Brooke that made Julie itch to slap her. It took all her willpower and then some not to let the girl see how she really felt.

"No, you and David go on. I'll be fine here alone."

The smile on Julie's face threatened to break. It was not in her nature to hide her emotions, but she was learning. Her relationship with Bob had taught her that, if nothing else.

David came down the stairs two at a time, looking tall and athletic and, to Julie's eyes, incredibly young. Could he really be planning to marry Brooke? She didn't think she could stand it!

"You're not coming with us?" David asked Brooke.

"No, I'm not really hungry."

"Castille's is famous for its Mexican food," Julie put in. "You might like it."

"No." Brooke's gaze was cool. "Thank you."

With a lighter heart Julie led David to her car, seating herself on the passenger side. She was glad Brooke wasn't coming, though it made her uneasy. The girl rarely let David out of her sight.

David drove expertly through the lunch-hour traffic, handing the keys to Julie's T-bird to the parking attendant at Castille's. Julie clasped his hand as they walked to the door, knowing she was winning his trust, feeling a little guilty that she shamelessly used his love for fancy cars to her own advantage. David had practically drooled over the T-bird. If it was up to her she would just give him the car—but it had been a gift from Bob.

"Two for lunch," she told the maître d'.

Wicker chairs were grouped around glass-topped tables, piñatas hung from the ceiling, and waitresses in flounced, brightly colored skirts that showed layers of ruffled petticoats weaved between the tables and chairs. A mariachi band was strolling from room to room and the noise level reflected the restaurant's popularity.

"I don't think I'm dressed right," David said uncomfortably, looking down at his jeans.

"You're perfect," Julie assured him as they were led to a table in the center of the room.

"I wish Brooke had come," David said.

She glanced up from her menu. "She must have had things she wanted to do without us."

"What things?"

Julie shrugged. "Don't worry about it. Let's just enjoy our lunch and have a good time. We'll be back before Brooke has time to get lonely."

Brooke slammed the oak cupboard shut with all her strength, rattling Julie's dishes. Damn it! David had just gone ahead without so much as a kiss good-bye. Julie was winning!

Desperate, she ran upstairs, relieved to find David's keys on his dresser. She'd been so sure David would take the hint and stay home with her. They could have been in bed together by now, but no, he had to keep his lunch date with Mommy Dear.

Snatching up the keys, Brooke hurried downstairs, ran out to David's car, and fired the ignition. After several aborted attempts the engine hiccupped and caught, and she reversed with a grind of gears out of the drive.

Storm clouds gathered in her dark eyes. The time had come. No more pussyfooting around. Julie Anderson was in for the fight of her life.

Neil knocked on the door to Amanda's house, straightening the lapels of his jacket. He had to fight the urge to see if any of the neighbors were watching. Then he shook himself. For all anyone knew he and Amanda had just started a relationship. There was no reason to be paranoid, no reason at all.

When Amanda opened the door Neil was shocked. Her face was pale, her lips colorless. Prudently, he waited until he was inside before drawing her into his arms. "Oh, sweetheart, I didn't know how this had gotten you down."

Amanda tucked her face into his comforting shoulder. "I'm so glad you came. I've been so scared."

"Scared?"

"Neil, I have these terrible dreams. There's Charles, pointing at me, judging me. I'm sure he knows about us, Neil. And he blames me for everything."

"Charles is dead," he said gently.

"Not to me. Not when I'm home alone here at night."

Soft sobs shook her and Neil felt the front of his shirt dampen with her tears. He stroked her head, crooning soft words of comfort, all the time watching the clock. Though he knew it was selfish and thoughtless, he couldn't help wishing Amanda would get over her self-doubts so they could just take up where they'd left off. He needed her. Needed her warm love and support. Needed her to help push aside his fear of Jimmy Sentra—at least for a little while.

"Amanda." His mouth searched for hers. He tasted the saltiness of her tears.

"Oh, Neil. I'm such a mess," she moaned, swiping at her eyes. "I don't know what to do."

"Here. Come here," he invited gently, leading her to the room off the kitchen, where a deluxe mirrored bar stood behind a leather couch and chair. He pushed a panel on the back wall, his reflection distorting as the mirror slid inward, revealing a shelf stocked with the finest names in liquor. He poured them each a healthy shot from the first bottle he encountered.

"These dreams . . ." Amanda began again.

"Forget the dreams. They'll pass. You just need to heal."

"I'm afraid." She accepted the drink, but didn't lift it to her lips. "What if they don't go away?"

"They will." He clinked her glass, swallowed half of his drink at once, made a face, then let out a heavy sigh. Gently, he took her hand in his and pulled her down on the couch beside him.

"I can't wait, Neil. I called Dr. Horton again and made an appointment for later today."

"You *what?*" Neil nearly dropped his drink.

"I told you, didn't I, that I'd gone to see Dr. Laura Horton before?"

He was shaken. "When?"

"I don't know. Before Charles died, but I was afraid to talk to her—"

"Amanda." He set his glass on the coffee table, his mind racing. "What did you tell her about us?"

"Nothing . . . then."

If he had thought his world was crumbling around him before, now he knew it was. Amanda had talked to Laura! His career—all he had left—hung on a thin wire. "You told her something later?" he questioned faintly.

Amanda shook her head. "Not yet. I'll talk to her this afternoon."

"No, Amanda. You can't see her. You can't tell her where you were the night Charles died."

"But I—"

"No." Neil shushed her lips with his finger. "It'll kill both our reputations. My clientele will drop me and you'll be labeled a heartless adulteress."

Her lips parted on a moan.

"Don't you see, it'll only make things worse." He carefully wrapped her fingers around her glass. "Here. Drink up. We've got to work this out ourselves, Amanda. You don't need a psychiatrist."

"She seemed so understanding," she said weakly.

"I know, sweetheart. Really I do. But I'm a doctor, too, don't forget. Haven't I always been straight with you about Charles's health? I wouldn't lie to you. And discussing those dreams with Laura will only make you think of them all the more."

"I couldn't stand that," Amanda murmured, taking a sip.

"That's right. Go ahead. Drink it all. If you need help, I'll help you. We'll start right now. How do you feel?"

She shivered. "Scared."

Neil put his arm over her shoulder, cradling her close.

"Better?"

"Mmm."

"Now stop thinking about going to see Dr. Horton. Don't worry." He kissed her neck, swallowing his own fears, and murmured, "Dr. Neil Curtis will cure all your ills . . ."

The Castille's maître d' looked Brooke up and down, thinking that with a proper haircut and some tending to the slim brunette woman could be downright stunning. But when Brooke looked contemptuously down her nose at him he quickly reversed his opinion. "Miss?" he said coolly.

"I'm looking for someone," she said, then caught sight of Julie sitting at a table in the center of the room, alone.

Where was David? Seeing the look of love shining poignantly from Julie's eyes, Brooke gritted her teeth, knowing who had to be on the receiving end. She followed Julie's gaze, but to her surprise it wasn't David Julie was watching, it was another man.

His back was to Brooke, but she could see his brown hair, the broad width of his shoulders, his lean hips and expensive clothes. Who was he?

David walked into view at that moment, carefully balancing two frothy margaritas. He'd been to the bar, Brooke realized, and not wanting to be spotted just yet, she slid back out of sight. The maître d's brows lifted but she ignored him.

The dark-haired man suddenly rose. As soon as he stood, Julie's eyes dropped to her plate.

Brooke watched this exchange with interest. Then the man walked out of the restaurant and right in front of Brooke. She gave him a brilliant smile, but he barely noticed her. With his hand on the door he glanced back once, at Julie, then he thrust through the double doors, a cool breath of fall swirling inside as he exited.

Brooke quickly crossed into the restaurant dining room, stopping by the man's table. She read the name on the credit card receipt. Doug Williams.

Thoughtfully, she glanced back toward the reception area. Doug Williams. A handsome man. Someone who mattered to Julie. She was so lost to her own plans it was several seconds before she realized her name was being called.

"Brooke!"

It was David, a grin splitting his face. He was standing by his table, signaling her. His eagerness did a lot to revive her floundering ego, but when Brooke glanced at Julie there was no animation in her pretty features.

"I was just wondering who that man was," Brooke said as she came to their table, pleased that David had pulled her chair back. Though she was determined to get him out from under his mother's influence, it was nice that he'd learned some of the finer points of gentlemanliness all the same.

"What man?" David looked around the restaurant.

"That handsome dark-haired one. You know, Julie. The one you were looking at."

Julie met her gaze blandly. "I don't know who you mean."

"You were looking right at him. And he

looked at you, too. He's tall, attractive, kind of muscular. He had on a tan sport coat. Is he a friend of yours?"

Julie didn't answer.

"Maybe the waitress knows," Brooke suggested, and called the one clearing Doug's table over before either Julie or David could protest. "The man who was seated at that table. We think we know him. Could you tell us his name?"

The waitress fumbled with the credit card slip. "Doug Williams."

"Thanks." Brooke was almost afraid to look at Julie, certain the triumph she felt would be spread across her face.

"Doug Williams," David repeated, dazed.

Julie picked up her margarita, seething inside. Across the top of the glass she met Brooke's eyes, wanting more than anything to wipe the smugness off her face. "Doug and I don't talk to each other anymore, David," she said firmly. "We've each made new lives. Brooke was mistaken." She took another sip of her drink.

Bull's-eye! So she'd been right!

Silence fell over the table. With the kind of instinctive timing she'd learned at the school of hard knocks, Brooke didn't press her advantage. She sighed and looked at David's margarita. "Think you could get me one of those? I'm parched."

"Let me." Julie's voice was cold as she pulled a ten-dollar bill from her wallet. "I could do with another myself."

The rain poured down in opaque sheets. Susan could hardly see across the road to the houses on the other side. Their lights were wavy blurs, their outlines indistinct shapes that melded together into a background of dark gray.

"Damn."

She walked away from the window. Greg was late again. Late? Hah! That was being kind. She had no idea what his work schedule really was. Every time she tried to talk to him he cut her off with his customary, "Sorry, Susan. It'll have to wait. I've got to get to the hospital."

Did he think she was a complete moron? He'd never worked so hard before in all the years they'd been married. It was something else, and she didn't for a minute believe it was because he was helping pick up on Dr. Neil Curtis's workload.

There had to be another woman.

Susan poured herself a cup of coffee, stared down at it in distaste, then added a stiff shot of bourbon. She made up her mind. If he wasn't home by ten tonight she was going down to the hospital, or his office, wherever he was, and find out just what the hell was going on. If there was a woman involved, she would deal with her, too.

Sighing, she seated herself at the kitchen table. She'd never really thought about life without Greg; he'd been there so long she'd never had to. But she felt an uneasy prickle on her scalp and knew it was from her own fear. She was losing him.

Watching the clock go around was sheer torture. Eight. Eight-thirty. Nine. Nine-thirty. Nine forty-five.

Susan poured herself another cup of coffee, added more bourbon, and tried not to listen to her jangling nerves. *Fifteen minutes, Greg.*

That's all you've got. Fifteen minutes.

She was pushing her arms through her coat and reaching for her umbrella when lights suddenly shone through the picture window. She was standing in the exact same position when Greg entered through the back door, shaking rain off his coat.

"Susan," he said, surprised.

He would have normally walked right past her, but tonight he hesitated, wondering why she was putting on her coat. He waited, half angry, half impatient.

"So you came home," Susan said flatly. "I wondered if you would."

"What are you talking about? I always come home."

"Oh, sure." She set the umbrella down carefully. "Sometimes at eight, sometimes at ten, sometimes after midnight. But you're right, you always come home."

Greg ran a hand through his rain-soaked hair. "Look, I don't have time for this tonight. I'm tired. And I've still got a ton of work to do."

"Neil's work?"

"Yes, Neil's work. And mine."

"Who is she, Greg?"

The question came out so softly it took him a beat to realize what she was really asking. The look on his face said she was crazy, but Susan was through with lies.

"Tell me." She stood like a statue. "Right now."

It was her utter quiet that made Greg realize this was no ordinary fight. Susan was not a woman to hide her feelings well. When she was angry, she was enraged; when she was happy—

which was much too seldom—she was ecstatic. But the expressionless woman in front of him was a stranger.

"There is no one but you," he told her calmly, watching her. "I really am busy. I've been trying to talk to Neil for weeks about this without much success. He keeps putting me off. But I'm going to corner him tomorrow. Things at the office have hit crisis point."

It was true. Today Greg had learned there wasn't enough money in the checking account to pay Roxie's salary. He'd had to pay it out of his own pocket.

But Susan was past listening. Her instincts told her she was fighting a rival of flesh and blood. "Okay, Greg. You don't have to tell me tonight. I'll find out all on my own."

"I told you, there isn't anyone else," he answered angrily. "Enough is enough, Susan."

"Is that why you don't sleep with me anymore? Is that why you're always tired and disinterested? Don't lie to me, Greg!"

"I'm not—"

But she had turned on her heel and his words were cut off by the harsh slamming of the bedroom door. Greg ground his teeth together, but a part of him was glad. Glad he didn't have to come up with excuses about why he didn't want to make love to her.

The truth was painfully simple: Susan just didn't interest him anymore.

The rain was incessant. It poured off the eaves for days, soaking the ground, sending tiny rivers flooding down the driveway and into the street.

Brooke restlessly paced the hardwood floors

of the study, her eyes constantly turning to the paned windows, watching the rain streak down. David's relationship with Julie had gone past annoying to downright scary. She sensed that she was on the verge of being thrown over. And for whom? His *mother*, for God's sake!

Uttering a sound of anxiety, Brooke bit into her bottom lip. She wasn't down for the count yet. There was still one card left up her sleeve: Doug Williams.

She'd learned a lot about Doug over the past few days, interjecting an innocent question here, an off-hand query there. The man owned a restaurant and bar in the center of Salem called Doug's Place. With a little luck, Brooke could find out all she needed to know about him there.

David, Julie, and Bob had gone out for dinner together. Brooke had declined, vainly hoping once more that David would stay with her. It had been far too long since she'd curled up in the security of his arms, reveled in the touch and feel of him.

And she wouldn't get the chance again tonight. She knew the scenario well by now: after dinner they would all go into the family room and talk and play cards. What a bore.

With a scowl meant for the world in general, Brooke stole upstairs, found David's keys again, and let herself out the front door. Resentment curled inside her. They probably wouldn't even realize she'd left.

She arrived at Doug's Place just as the singer, a handsome dark Frenchman, began a set of songs. Seating herself at the bar, Brooke feigned deep interest in him while in actual fact her eyes were darting around the room, checking over all the employees for a possible source of information.

The bartender himself seemed the most likely soul. He looked to be in his forties, with the faintest touch of gray at his temples and a face that had seen the world. Brooke figured him to be the man who'd been there the longest.

She gave him her most winning smile and lifted her glass. "I guess I could use another drink."

"I guess you could. What would you like?"

She leaned her elbows on the bar, letting the gap in the front of her blouse open a little wider. "What would you suggest?"

"Well, I don't know. How about a Dan Smythson special?"

"Your creation?"

"Of course."

"I'd love one," Brooke said, slowly drawing her bangs away from her eyes. She watched him put together a drink that had at least three kinds of alcohol and told herself to sip it down slowly or she'd never get what she came for. "Thank you," she said, when the tall, frosted glass was placed in front of her.

"It's on the house," he said.

Brooke had been reaching for her purse. Now she set it back down and cocked her head to one side. "Well, thank you again. Are you the owner?"

"No. But what he doesn't know won't hurt him."

They laughed together. "I've seen him, y'know," Brooke said, sliding a provocative glance from the corner of her eye. "He looks pretty good."

"Doug?" Dan Smythson's male ego couldn't take it. Begrudgingly, he said, "He's all right if you like that type."

"What type is that?" Brooke licked a drop of liquor from her lips, pleased at the way Dan's eyes followed her every move.

"Not *your* type."

She didn't take offense. Instead she lowered her lashes, the hint of a smile at the corner of her mouth. "Maybe you're right. I suppose he goes for the schoolteacher type. The kind that doesn't know how to have a really good time."

Smythson leaned on the bar. "Something like that. Although I've never seen Doug with anyone since his wife died." He frowned, as if his words had brought something else to mind.

"I didn't know he was married."

"Well, it wasn't exactly made in heaven, if you know what I mean. I think he always fancied his wife's daughter more."

Brooke did some quick thinking. "You mean Julie," she said nonchalantly.

"Yeah, Julie. Hey, did you come here to talk about Doug all night, or what?"

Dan Smythson had a tie tucked into a bar apron. DOUG'S PLACE was printed across it in white letters, and Brooke reached forward, grabbed it, and pulled him closer. "That's right," she purred, forming a silent kiss with her lips, but when he leaned forward to touch her mouth she slid off the bar stool. "Maybe next time, you'll get lucky, but don't count on it."

Sauntering away, Brooke enjoyed her fleeting moment of power. But was it so fleeting? Dan Smythson had armed her with far more than she'd bargained for.

* * *

The bedroom door was stuck and Trish kicked her foot against it several times, muttering under her breath. If it wasn't that she needed the privacy she would leave it open all the time, but that was impossible. As it was, she and Michael were like a couple of Keystone Cops, turning this way and that, trying to avoid one another. It was silly, but necessary, and Trish found his blushing gallantry endearing.

Such a change from what she'd been used to.

She checked the clock. Michael wasn't due home from work yet. Funny, how she'd come to depend so much on his friendship. In ways they were like a well-seasoned couple, planning meals together, checking what was on tomorrow's agenda, playing board games. Without a television they spent hours over Monopoly and Clue, and Trish had quickly learned that Michael, for all his "aw shucks, ma'am" manners, was lightning swift on the uptake. He'd beaten her more often than not.

Trish looked in the cupboards and wrinkled her nose. It looked like they were having toasted cheese sandwiches again. But it wouldn't be long before she started at Bo Peep's, and then she could offer more than the small portion of her savings she was forced to use each week.

She heard a knock on the door and nearly jumped from her skin. Who would be coming to see her? Only her family knew where she was.

Cracking the door, a cold knot formed in her stomach when she saw who was on the other side. "Well, hello, Jack," she said slowly. "What are you doing here?"

"I just came over to make sure my baby girl

was all right. Now open the door and let me see for myself."

Trish hesitated, not knowing what to do. Her every instinct told her to keep him out.

He put a heavy hand on the door and pushed. "If you don't let me in, I might think somethin's wrong, honey," he said softly. "Come on, now. Don't make me break it down."

She backed up and Jack walked into the tiny living room. It was an effort, but she managed to keep from looking at the clock. Michael wouldn't be back for a good hour anyway.

"Where's that young friend of yours?"

"He's—he's at work still. He should be home any minute."

Jack gave her a long look. He walked down the hall, twisted the knob on the bedroom door, found it stuck, gave Trish a searching glance, then kicked it in. The door shuddered and slammed against the opposite wall. Seeing her clothes tossed over the bed, he asked, "And where does he sleep?"

"On the couch."

"Uh-huh." Jack came back into the living room, standing so close to Trish she could feel his breath on her face. She had to fight not to turn away. He brushed the hair off her forehead. "So how is my baby, really?"

"I'm not your baby, Jack," Trish said, looking at the floor. Her heart was pounding wildly.

"Sure y'are. Come here." He grabbed her hand and pulled her unwillingly toward the couch. "This where your friend sleeps? This couch?"

Trish didn't answer. She'd always been afraid of Jack on a subliminal level, but lately her fear

You can now order previous titles of *Soaps & Serials*™ Books by mail!

Just complete the order form, detach, and send together with your check or money order payable to:

Soaps & Serials™
120 Brighton Road, Box 5201
Clifton, NJ 07015-5201

- - - - - - - - - - - - - - - - - -

Please <u>circle</u> the book #'s you wish to order:

The Young and The Restless	1	2	3	4	5	6	7	8	9
Days of Our Lives......	1	2	3	4	5	6	7	8	9
Guiding Light	1	2	3	4	5	6	7	8	9
Another World	1	2	3	4	5	6	7	8	9
As The World Turns....	1	2	3	4	5	6	7	8	9
Dallas™................	1	2	3	4	5	6	7	8	9
Knots Landing™	1	2	3	4	5	6	7	8	9
Capitol™..............	1	2	3	4	NOT AVAILABLE				

Each book is $2.50 ($3.50 in Canada).

Total number of books circled _____ × price above = $ _____

Sales tax (CT and NY residents only) $ _____

Shipping and Handling $ _____ .95

Total payment enclosed $ _____
(check or money orders only)

Name _____

Address _____ Apt# _____

City _____

State _____ Zip _____

Telephone (_____) _____

Area code   DOOL 9 had increased. Where before he'd made only suggestive comments, covert moves, she sensed that something had changed.

"Jack, I—"

"What's the matter? You don't like the questions?"

Trish tried to ease away from him. "No . . ."

"Now, come here."

Jack's grip had tightened. She wasn't certain if he even realized it. Heart pounding, Trish sat still and stiff, repulsed and afraid.

His hand stroked her hair and she flinched. She couldn't help it. But Jack saw and his expression turned ugly. "You don't appreciate me, little girl," he said. "You never have. I took your mom and you in, y'know. When you was still a kid. Now you're grown and actin' too good for anybody. It's a shame."

"Jack . . ." Trish actually felt faint. "Why don't you just go home? Mom's probably waiting."

His laugh was harsh. "Sure. She's always waitin'. Waitin' and waitin'. Not like you, huh? You just took off to start this new life all on your own. After all I done for you."

All Trish's fears, fears that had been simmering just below the surface for years, came boiling upward. She'd wanted to get out of the house because of Jack. She'd been afraid of him. And she was afraid of him now.

She jerked away from him and tried to stand. Lightning fast, he grabbed her wrist and yanked her back down. She inhaled, fighting for breath, but his heavy lips found hers. With a scream in her throat she struggled in earnest, clawing and fighting, but he was a big man. When she was finally able to wrench her mouth away, the scream tore out, high and wild.

The back door crashed in. "Trish?" Michael demanded, scared.

"Mike—" Tears filled her eyes, cutting off her words. But Michael heard and suddenly he was standing at the foot of the couch, his face slowly draining of color.

Jack quickly released Trish and rolled to his feet. Caught in the act he could hardly bluff his way out. Instead he lowered his head, his shoulders tense and rounded.

Michael reacted on instinct. Size meant nothing to him. All he wanted to do was pummel Jack Clayton for all he was worth and damn the consequences. Adrenaline was pumping through his veins like molten fire. He balanced himself on his feet and waited for Clayton, teeth bared, hands clenched; he wanted to wrap his hands around Clayton's fat neck and strangle him.

Chapter Six

Tragedy

Jack took one look at Michael and changed position. "Well, now," he said, straightening. "I guess I misunderstood what my baby's been tellin' me. She said she wanted a man, not a boy."

"Get out," Michael said through clenched teeth.

Clayton raised his hands. "Okay, okay." His cowardice painted a smile on his beefy face. "Just a misunderstandin', now."

Michael didn't speak. He stared the older man down until Jack finally headed for the door. But as soon as the door shut behind him, sweat broke out on Michael's back. He sank on the couch beside Trish. "You all right?"

"Michael . . . Michael . . ." she said brokenly, burrowing her face against his neck.

He had never been so close to a fight before, had never felt the need to satisfy his anger by slamming his fist into another man's face. But he felt that need now—and it was difficult to shrug off.

"Trish," he said, wrapping his arms around

her, letting his rage cool. *Jack Clayton will get his, someday,* he reminded himself grimly. *I just hope I'm around to give it to him.*

"He tried to—"

"I know."

"There was nothing I could do. I was so afraid." She sniffed and attempted to pull herself together but ended up holding him even tighter. "You're all I've got. I don't even really have a mom anymore."

Michael closed his eyes. Reaction was setting in. He felt weak and liquid. And he felt Trish in his arms, warm and trusting and smelling of soap and light perfume.

With senses still heightened from his skirmish with Clayton, he realized how little it would take on Trish's part to make living with her unbearable.

While she cried and held him, Michael fought his own emotions, thinking in disgust how he was no better than Trish's stepfather. He was honest enough to know he wanted her in much the same way. He cared about her, maybe even loved her, and now he wished he'd never allowed her to move in.

How much longer could he keep his feelings to himself?

Brooke lay on David's bed, flipping through a magazine. She glanced toward the bathroom, wondering how long it would take before he got out of the shower. Should she be lying naked on the bed when he came out? Or did she have enough time to steal one of Julie's negligees? If David wouldn't come to his senses by simple reasoning, she would make him remember what he'd been missing. Then he would surely see what a shallow, selfish woman his mother was, while, she—Brooke—was eager and loving and warm.

Hearing the shower door open, she quickly took off her dress and kicked it off to one side. She didn't have time to remove her slip so she lay on the bed and smoothed it around her—cream lace on a blue satin cover. Propping her head on her hand, she let one nyloned leg dangle over the edge, catching the toe of a bone-colored pump, swinging it gently to and fro.

The bathroom door opened and David came out, a towel slung over his hips, while he rubbed his hair dry with another.

All Brooke's plans fell apart as she gaped at him. "You cut your hair!" she cried. "She got you to cut your hair!"

"I've walked by that men's hairdressing place a hundred times. The one near the grocery center. I just felt like cutting it."

He walked past her, yanked open a drawer, and pulled out some neatly pressed trousers. Brooke's shoe dropped to the floor with a clatter. She sat straight, burning up inside. "You're not the same David I came to Salem with. You're Julie Anderson's son!"

"That's right." The drawer slammed shut. "Quit making such a big deal about it."

"You don't even want me anymore! I could stand stark naked in front of you and it wouldn't make any difference!"

"For God's sake, give me time, Brooke!" David suddenly exploded. "You want everything so fast. *Right now.* Life doesn't work that way."

"It does if you want it to." She grabbed her

dress and jerked it over her head. Struggling with the zipper, she said, "You could make love to me right now. Here in your room. Just like we used to. But you won't!"

"Brooke . . ." He gestured to the door. "Julie and Bob are right downstairs."

"So what? You didn't use to care what people thought. Why not give good old Mom something to think about? You're an adult, David. Act like one."

His eyes narrowed and his chin jutted out stubbornly in a way Brooke knew meant he'd been pushed too far. "Sounds like good advice for you, too," he growled.

Brooke crossed the room and slid her arms around his waist. "David, let's not fight. I'm sorry I've been so nasty. It's just—"

"My mother." David deliberately pulled her hands away from him, holding her at arm's length. "I don't want to hurt her any more than I already have."

Brooke's cooling temper did an abrupt reversal. "Hurt *her*? She's the one who's hurt people. You know she's been carrying on an affair with Doug Williams, don't you? That was no chance meeting at the restaurant the other day."

He thrust her away so fast she almost lost her balance.

Infuriated, Brooke threw caution to the wind, expanding her lie. "And that baby she's carrying? It isn't Bob's. It's Doug's! Everybody in town knows it but you!"

"Get out of here before I kill you, Brooke!"

David's rage was awesome to see. Belatedly she realized she'd gone too far. Without a word she did as he suggested, turning on her heel, tears of humiliation burning behind her eyes.

But she wouldn't cry. She wouldn't. And she was far from finished yet. Oh, no, the war wasn't over. David was hers. Now and forever. She was going to get him back if it took the rest of her life.

Julie stretched languidly, sensuously enjoying the smooth satin sliding against her flesh. It had been a long time since she'd had a dream about Doug; she'd repressed thoughts of him from her mind, and it had worked for her subconscious as well. Seeing him in the restaurant had triggered all kinds of memories, however, and she'd suddenly been unable to hold them back. Now they spilled into her dreams, making her life with Bob seem more of a sham than it already was.

She raised her head. The door to the other room was partially open and she could hear Bob in the bedroom, each deep breath ending on a half-snore. He wasn't awake yet. Good. She had a few more moments to savor her thoughts of Doug.

Quietly, Julie slid out of bed and curled up on the window seat. She looked outside, noticing that the rain had stopped and now the day looked crystal clear and cold. An ache came, out of nowhere, to fill her heart with unbearable sadness. She didn't love Bob. She loved Doug. But she was carrying Bob's child and Doug had made it perfectly clear he didn't love her anymore.

Julie's face darkened. Brooke had certainly done some pointed guessing there. She'd nearly turned David against her by just bringing up Doug's name. What a selfish, vindictive witch that girl was! Brooke would do anything to undermine Julie and get David back—even if it meant dragging Doug into the picture.

Sighing, Julie softly tiptoed into the bedroom, glanced at her sleeping husband, then headed for the bathroom. Something was going to have to give between herself and Bob, and Brooke was bound and determined to help push things along.

Locking the door, Julie ran a bath in the white porcelain tiled tub. She should really warn Doug, she thought as she settled into the hot water, bubbles tickling her chin. She should at least talk to him.

She knew where he lived, of course. It would be so easy just to drop by. She even had an excuse: her half sister, Hope, lived with him. Maybe it was time to show a little more interest in Hope. Maybe it was time to forget that her mother had stolen Doug from Julie and given him such a beautiful baby daughter.

Julie grimaced. When Addie had told her she was pregnant, it had been almost more than Julie could bear. As a consequence, she'd never gotten close to Hope. But now, well, she recognized she'd made a few mistakes herself. Managing to forgive her mother had been tough, but there was no sense in continuing to blame poor, innocent, little Hope for a situation created by her parents.

"Julie?" The doorknob twisted as Bob's voice sounded through the panels.

"I'll be out in a minute. I'm taking a bath."

"Okay. Take your time."

She heard his footsteps recede and hated herself a little. Why couldn't she love Bob? It would make life so much simpler. Instead she thought of Doug and let her head fill with foolish pipe-dreams.

Blowing bubbles off her hand, Julie resolved to forget about Doug once and for all and count her blessings right here at home.

An hour later, as Julie stood in the kitchen, morning sunshine slanted through the window blinds. With her resolution still ringing in her ears, Julie followed her heart and not her head. "Doug?" she said into the receiver, winding the phone cord around her finger.

"Julie?" Doug didn't try to hide his surprise.

"I—I was calling about Hope. I haven't seen her in a while and I was wondering if it would be all right . . . sometime . . . if I stopped by?"

She winced, hearing how breathless she sounded. Good Lord, he would have to know how much she still loved him!

There was a marked hesitation. "Well, sure, Julie. Anytime."

He doesn't want me, Julie cried inside, but she'd gone too far to give up now. "How about tomorrow afternoon? If you can't be there, maybe you could let the sitter know?"

"I'll be there." She could almost hear him thinking. "I've got tomorrow afternoon off."

"Oh, great." She had no idea what else to say. "I'll see you then."

"Until tomorrow," Doug agreed.

Replacing the receiver, she felt the fast pounding of her heart. Her conscience nagged her, but Julie ignored it. She turned around, a smile forming on her lips.

David was standing in the doorway.

"Oh! Hi. I didn't hear you," she said lamely.

Without a word, David crossed to the refrigerator, pulling out a pitcher of orange juice. He didn't meet her eyes. "Who was that on the phone?"

Realizing she'd been caught, Julie wasn't about to compound her error with a lie. "Doug Williams. He is Hope's father, you know. And Hope's my sister."

David poured a glass of juice, still refusing to look at her. "You don't have to be so defensive, Mom."

"I'm not defensive. I'm just telling you what you heard." There was silence between them and Julie strove to set things right again. "Would you like some breakfast? Eggs and bacon? Pancakes?"

"No, thanks." He drank the juice down in one long draft. "Brooke and I are going out for an early lunch. We're gonna have to leave Salem soon, or find some kind of employment. We can't keep living off you."

"You could work for Bob at his construction business," Julie suggested, desperate to keep him with her.

"We'll see."

He walked out of the kitchen and she had to force herself not to follow and beg him to believe her. She knew how David felt about Doug. Why, oh why, had she ever called him?

Even as she lamented her foolishness, deep in her heart Julie knew she wouldn't change tomorrow's meeting. She'd been dying a little inside each day, loving Doug so much it hurt. She had to see him. She had to reaffirm that it was over between them.

And if it wasn't? Well, she'd cross that bridge when she came to it.

* * *

David inhaled the crisp fall air until it hurt his lungs. Even then he held his breath, punishing himself. Then he exhaled in a rush and walked from the front porch to the garage.

He flipped on the light and there was Julie's snow-white Thunderbird. Sliding his hand over its smooth finish, he asked himself what he was doing. Since overhearing the phone call between his mother and Doug the day before, he'd been in a state of anxiety he couldn't shake. And it was all Brooke's fault. Planting those terrible notions in his head. Every time he thought of Julie with Doug he wanted to die.

Pressing his hands against his head, he waited until the dreadful images of them together disappeared. He tried to rationalize his feelings, knowing he was overreacting but unable to help himself. Doug had been a source of friction between him and his mother for as long as David could remember. He blamed Doug for all the trauma of his youth. To think of Julie with him again was more than he could bear.

He heard his mother's footsteps on the front porch and straightened. When she came around the corner of the garage she stopped, surprised. "David. What are you doing here?"

She was dressed in a blue shift that hid her pregnancy. A white cowl-necked sweater looked fluffy and soft around her neck. Her eyes sparkled. Her perfume reached across the space between them and made David feel slightly sick.

She'd done all this for Doug.

"I was wondering if you could drop me off at the Salem Racquet Club," he asked in a tight voice. He'd done his research. He knew Doug Williams didn't live far from the club.

"Sure. Is Brooke going?"

"No. She's resting."

He wasn't about to tell Julie that he and Brooke weren't speaking since their argument. He had to work some things out before he could confide in his mother.

"You want to drive?" She held out the keys, her smile mixed with perplexity as she tried to read his mind.

"Sure."

It took an extraordinary amount of concentration for David to reverse the smooth-running T-bird. His mind was elsewhere. Filled with thousands of self-doubts and recriminations. He was going to spy on his mother!

Just because Brooke had poisoned his mind.

But he couldn't stop now.

At the Racquet Club, Julie slid over to the driver's seat. "David, are you all right?" she asked, rolling the window down. "You look kind of pale."

He was standing beside the car, his hands on the door, looking down at the burnished crown of Julie's hair. Impulsively, he leaned over and kissed the top of her head.

Smiling, she asked quizzically, "David?"

"I'm fine. Listen, I'll catch you later."

"Do you want me to pick you up in an hour or two?"

"No. I'll call." He backed away and waved, then turned, thrusting his hands in his pocket, walking up the steps to the front door of the club.

There was a cold feeling in his lower back. A

premonition. His hand was on the knob but he hesitated as he heard the T-bird roar away.

He drew in another breath, tugged the collar of his coat close to his neck. In an instant he was back down the steps, sprinting after the white car just cresting the hill.

The sight of Doug's house brought an aching feeling to the back of Julie's throat. Slowly, she drove the last few yards, easing to a stop across the road. For a few moments she sat quietly, listening to the engine tick and cool. Then she let herself out, screwed up her courage, and walked across the street and up the sidewalk to the front door.

A horn blasted. Julie whirled around. Doug's gleaming red Corvette pulled into the drive.

He switched off the ignition and climbed out. "Hi," he said, lightly closing the door behind him.

"Hi, yourself. Or should I say, 'Long time no see'?"

Doug's smile was self-deprecatory as he leaned against the hood. "How would, 'I've missed you terribly' rate?"

"Low." Julie turned away, feeling hot tears fill her throat. "You were the one who didn't want to see *me*, remember?"

"Did you really come to see Hope?"

"Yes." She fought for control. "And no."

"Julie . . ."

"Don't, Doug. Not unless you mean it this time."

Her shoulders stiffened as she heard his footsteps on the sidewalk but she didn't turn around. He was right behind her. She could hear his breathing. "Don't you realize that I only wanted to do what was best for the baby?"

Blinking, she asked, "You knew I was pregnant?"

"Yes."

"How? I'd just found out myself."

"I overheard Dr. Curtis telling you the news in his office. I couldn't let you divorce Bob then."

Julie's head spun. "Oh, Doug . . ." she whispered.

"It seemed like the noble thing to do at the time," he added with a trace of bitterness. "But it's been hell."

Both of them were so wrapped up in their feelings neither noticed the young man standing near the maple tree in Doug's front yard. David remained perfectly still. He didn't want to believe his eyes or his ears. Though the day was bright it had turned gray and dismal to him. His mouth was dry. His heart thudded a slow, painful beat. Brooke was right. Julie and Doug were having an affair. For all he knew, the baby might be Doug's after all.

He saw Doug lift his hands, as if to cradle Julie's shaking shoulders, but he didn't touch her. She turned around and gazed into his eyes, her own shimmering with huge, crystal tears.

"I love you," she said. "You know that."

Doug's hand lightly traced her face. "I've never stopped loving you, Julie. Ever. I never could."

David reached backward, his hand connecting with the rough bark of the tree. Julie and Doug. *Brooke was right!*

"What are we going to do?" she asked tremulously.

"I don't know."

David was breathing hard. He fell back against the tree. Inside, he'd known all along. His mother was a fraud.

Julie and Doug. They were close to the front door, too absorbed in each other to notice him. David turned glazed eyes from them to the gleaming Corvette. It beckoned, shining and scarlet in the bright cold sunshine.

His mind a blank, David stepped across the withered maple leaves to the car, the noise loud and crackling. Julie and Doug looked around.

"David . . ." Julie took half a step toward him. Doug just stared, frowning.

The feel of the handle was clean and cool. The interior was black leather and smelled faintly of tobacco. David ran his palms over the steering wheel. The keys were in the ignition.

"David!"

Now Julie was running toward him. He turned the key. The engine purred. Slowly, he let out the clutch.

"David! What are you doing?" Julie's hands were reaching for the door, scrabbling for a hold.

Easily, smoothly, the car glided backward, out of the driveway. Doug was running after him.

"Hey!" he was shouting. "Hey you! Get out of that car!"

David, very calmly and succinctly, told Doug what he could do to himself.

Then he was driving fast. Past the houses that quickly became a colorful blur. Past the turn to the Racquet Club. Past the road to town. He was out on the highway. Pure and fast. Free.

* * *

"That's David!" Julie was screaming, racing after Doug. "That's my son."

"Where are your keys?" Doug demanded.

"H-here," she said, digging desperately through her purse. "Oh, God. Oh, my God."

Doug practically ripped them from her hands. "What the hell's the matter with him?" He leaped into the car. Julie stumbled around to the passenger side.

"It's you," she said, white-faced. "He saw me with you."

"Damn." He shot her a commiserating look and fired the engine. "We'll find him."

The T-bird's tires groaned as Doug made a tight U-turn and followed in David's wake. Julie's hands were gripped around the edge of her seat. "I'm afraid," she said.

"So am I," Doug answered grimly.

The Corvette handled like a dream. It hugged corners, tires screeching, the wind screaming through the open window. Cold air burned his face but David didn't feel it. He just drove. As far and fast as he could.

Julie and Doug. Why hadn't he guessed from the beginning? Nothing had changed. He'd trusted her, and again learned she had feet of clay.

She is nothing, he thought. *I am nothing*.

David saw the signpost for River Road and shifted down, the Corvette squealing and shuddering as he stamped on the brake. He made the corner, his right tire bumping over the shoulder, snapping a dry tree limb in half. Then he shifted again, his foot squeezing down on the accelerator until the car bounced back on the highway.

The road was winding and hilly. It took all David's concentration to keep up speed without crashing. He poured on the gas, his teeth gritting and head pounding.

Julie and Doug. What else was there left?

The road leveled out, a straight black ribbon heading toward the river. David saw a bridge outlined against the sky. The bridge at Kelley Point.

The river lay quiet and dark on either side of the bridge. David slowed to a stop, engine idling. He didn't know how long he sat there but finally he began backing up, his gaze focused on the end of the straightaway.

"That's him," Julie whispered, dying with fright, but as Doug tore around the corner she saw it was a different red sports car, not even close to resembling Doug's.

"He had to come this way," Doug muttered. "He was going too fast to go back to town."

"Then where is he?"

"He must have turned down River Road," Doug muttered, yanking the T-bird around in a swirl of dirt.

"But River Road's so narrow and winding." Julie fretfully pressed her nose against the window. "What if . . . ?"

"Don't say it. Don't even think it. We'll find him."

They drove fast, Doug handling the car like the expert driver he was. There was no traffic, only the onrushing wind as it shook the rust and orange-colored leaves from the maples and poplars along the road.

"There!" Julie shouted, seeing the red Corvette at the end of the straightaway that led to the bridge.

It was as if her shout were a signal to David, though he couldn't possibly have heard her. The Corvette's back wheels began churning, its engine whining into high gear. As the T-bird skimmed around the last corner the Corvette took off in a wild roar.

"David!" Julie screamed, blindly reaching for the door.

Doug stamped on the brake and the T-bird skidded around. In horror he watched the red car head for the bridge. Julie leapt from the car, running mindlessly. Chasing after her, Doug caught her arm, holding her, both of their gazes stricken, focused on the lone racing car.

It hit the edge of the bridge with a grinding thump, broke off a piece of concrete, then flew skyward, a brilliant scarlet arc. Then it plummeted, plunging into the water with a dreadful, heavy slap that sent Julie to her knees.

Then there was silence.

Chapter Seven

A Marriage of Convenience

A misting, unrelenting rain fell over the small congregation as they faced the gazebo in the Anderson backyard. Black umbrellas covered the heads of the mourners, and droplets of water ran off the edges to bead on the chrysanthemums that ringed the weathered steps. The mood was somber. No one could believe that David was dead.

Bob Anderson shifted his umbrella, making sure Julie was covered. He glanced uneasily at her white face. She'd barely said three words since Doug had brought her, screaming hysterically, through the front door the day before. Bob had immediately called Dr. Tom Horton, Julie's grandfather, and Tom had prescribed a sedative for her. So far Julie had refused to take it.

Thinking of Dr. Horton, Bob looked his way, seeing the deep lines of unhappiness that furrowed both his and his wife's faces. The entire Horton family grieved for David.

And they all grieved for Julie, too. Julie, who

had witnessed the accident that had taken her son's life.

The minister's soothing voice went on, like the quiet ripple of waves over sand. Bob lifted his eyes to the gray sky and tried not to think too much about how Doug had been the one to bring Julie home. It didn't matter why Julie had gone to Doug first. David was the reason they were all here. David was the reason Julie was now so close to collapse.

"Would anyone like to say a few words about David?" the minister asked, his face serene.

There weren't all that many people. Other than family, David hadn't had time to meet new friends. It was just as well. Julie had wanted this service in the backyard, a place she felt closest to her son. A huge crowd wouldn't have worked here.

"David was the most beautiful person on earth," a wavery feminine voice from the rear proclaimed. "I won't believe he's gone."

Bob felt his skin prickle as Brooke walked forward. His heart went out to her. In his anxiety over his wife, he'd forgotten she must be suffering as much as Julie.

She stopped by Bob's side. She had no umbrella and her dark hair was plastered to her head, her skin as gray as the overcast skies. In a moment of pure empathy Bob reached for her arm, drawing her under the shelter of his umbrella. He felt Julie tremble and he put his arm around both women.

Several people haltingly spoke up. It helped ease the tension created by Brooke's outburst. Bob felt someone's eyes upon them and turned to see Doug staring at Julie's bent head. Instinctively, Bob tightened his hold on both Julie and Brooke and was surprised to feel Brooke respond, clinging to him for support. *Poor Brooke,* he thought. She'd been treated so badly by all of them.

The memorial service ended several minutes later. Bob led Julie and Brooke back to the house and stood by as people expressed their sympathy. Laura and Bill talked to Julie and she managed to respond. Tom and Alice hugged her, murmuring condolences. More people passed by, one after another.

As Bob was shaking hands, he saw Doug lean over and speak to Julie, but she barely registered a response. *Maybe I'm overreacting,* he thought. This was hardly the time to start questioning her about why Doug had been behind the wheel of her T-bird.

He felt someone by his side and looked over his shoulder. Brooke was standing next to him. "He's not dead," she said in a tight whisper.

Bob pulled her to a corner of the room, around the buffet table and away from the others. With an eye on his wife to make certain she was still holding up, he said quietly, "I know it's hard to accept, Brooke. But he's dead. Julie saw him go over the bridge at Kelley Point."

"But they didn't find his body!"

"It makes no difference. He couldn't have survived the crash."

"He's not dead. He's coming back to me."

"Brooke," said Bob kindly, "they've already found the car. They'll find his body, too."

She wrenched away from him and ran out the French doors across the lawn to the gazebo. He could see her through the drizzling rain and thought how much harder accepting David's death was on her than it was on Julie. Julie had seen David go over the bridge. She hadn't questioned the outcome.

With a squaring of his tired shoulders Bob went back to stand by his wife and face the rest of the dreadful day.

The cash register opened with a familiar ding as Michael made change for the customer. He was counting to himself when he heard Lou come in from the garage. Glancing up, he saw the stooped man expertly shoot into his spittoon.

"Someone was here lookin' for you yesterday," said Lou.

The hairs on Michael's neck rose. "Oh?"

"Your girlfriend's daddy."

Michael turned and repeated blankly, "My girlfriend's daddy?"

"Jack Clayton."

Blood pounded through Michael's veins. He'd thought someone from Salem had found him. He should have known it was Trish's stepfather! "What did he want?"

"Didn't say. He was being casual like, y'know. Askin' about you on the side."

Michael shut the cash drawer. *Let him ask*, he thought violently. Inside, he still yearned to slam his fist into the older man's face.

"Look, kid." Lou grimaced and wiped a hand over his chin. "You work hard. You try hard. You're better than y'know."

Bowled over by these unsolicited compliments, Michael turned to stare at his employer. Lou was simply not the type. As if sensing how he felt, Lou shook his head and made a disparaging sound as he walked to the door. But he hesitated on his way out and added, "Jest watch your back, kid."

It was several seconds later, when the horn from the customer outside blasted impatiently, that Michael realized he'd been standing stock-still, lost in thought. Hurrying, he pulled his collar closer and ran through the rain to give the man his change.

Laura Horton peeled off her black dress and kicked off her shoes. Quickly she changed into a skirt and blouse and low-heeled brown pumps. David's memorial service had depressed her; the boy hadn't been much older than Michael. Silently empathizing with Julie, she checked her appointment schedule and hurried down the stairs to make certain she wasn't late for her two o'clock meeting.

At the bottom step she hesitated. Inside her book was a crossed-out appointment. Amanda Howard. It had bothered Laura that Amanda hadn't shown up after she'd scheduled. What had happened? she wondered. What was it Amanda found so frightening about keeping appointments with her?

Crossing to the phone, Laura dialed Amanda's number. The line rang and rang but no one answered. With a sigh, Laura hung up, snatched up her purse, and hurried out the door.

She resolved to call Amanda when she got to work.

Pouring herself a cup of coffee, Amanda looked through the window to the miserable weather outside. She felt terrible. Tired all the time. *If only Neil were here to help,* she thought. Then she'd be okay. She needed him so badly.

A board creaked in the other room. She whirled around, sloshing coffee from her cup. Her heart hammered. "Who's there?" she called, but her voice was barely above a whisper.

She waited in abject fear. Then slowly, carefully, she peered around the doorway into the den. Calling on the little courage she had left, Amanda crossed to the desk, opened the top drawer, and pulled out an unloaded pistol. Hands shaking, she held the gun in front of her, searching for the intruder.

But there was no one there. There never was.

Setting the cup on the counter, Amanda tried to soothe her ragged nerves. *I'm alone,* she thought. *And it's okay. It's the middle of the day. No one's here.*

Last night's dream came back to her in scattered fragments. Charles, grimly staring at her. Pointing.

Covering her face with her hands, Amanda moaned, "Oh, Neil. I need you. Please, please call me."

But the phone remained silent. Whatever was keeping Neil from her these past few days seemed to still be in effect. She prayed whatever it was would go away—and soon.

The parking spot with Dr. Greg Peters's name on it was empty when Neil wheeled into the lot. *Good.* He would be alone.

Sneaking through the back door, he unlocked his office and quietly turned on the lights. He didn't want Roxie to know he was here. He didn't want anyone to know.

Not that I'm doing anything wrong, he reminded himself. In actual fact, he was setting things right.

The checkbook for Curtis and Peters was in the bottom drawer. Neil pulled it out, making a face when he saw the last deposit. Greg had made it himself, with his own money. Neil had paid dearly for that one. The damn ingrate had practically read him the riot act for just taking money out of his own account.

"Well, we'll see who has to eat whose words," he muttered. Quickly withdrawing an envelope from his pocket, he yanked out the cashier's check from First Salem Financial Trust. He'd refinanced his Mercedes. He wasn't worried, though. He'd get enough money from Saturday's game to pay it off and then some.

For now, he would deposit the money, float his business a small loan, and get Greg off his back all in one fell swoop. He couldn't worry about where next week's paycheck was coming from. His sights were on Saturday. He had a feeling he was going to score big.

I've got to.

Neil immediately chastised himself for being so negative. He knew he was going to win. It was that simple.

"Everyone's gone," Bob said tenderly to his wife. "Why don't you lie down for a while."

Julie was standing at the window, staring through the afternoon gloom to the crushed grass and rain-beaten flowers surrounding the gazebo. She rubbed her arms, a slight tremor running just beneath her skin. "Lie down. Why? I couldn't sleep."

"It might relax you. Maybe you could take one of those sedatives Tom prescribed."

"No." She drew in an uneven breath. "I'm numb enough already."

"What about a cup of tea? I could make you one."

A long pause ensued, so long in fact that Bob didn't expect her to answer. Then she said, "Thank you, Bob. But I just want to be left alone."

Sighing, Bob sent a last concerned glance at his wife's silhouette and headed for the kitchen. He would make the tea anyway. She needed something. Hell, *he* needed something.

He stopped short upon encountering Brooke. She was seated at the table, staring straight ahead, her eyes huge. Without looking at him, she asked, "Do you want me to leave?"

"No. Of course not." Bob was horrified.

"I know I'm in the way. Just say the word and I'll go."

Feeling way out of his depth, Bob said, "Brooke, you're in shock. Why don't you do as I told Julie—go upstairs and lie down. You can stay here as long as you like. Let's just get through all this."

He put the kettle on the stove and heated some water. *I'm not good at this*, he thought. *I need help.*

He set a cup of tea in front of Brooke, then brought one to Julie. She was still standing by the window and looked blankly at the proffered cup when Bob held it out to her.

It was the last straw as far as Bob was concerned. He closed himself into the den. Dialing the phone, he impatiently counted the rings.

"Tom?" he said eagerly. "It's Bob. Look, I know Julie seems like she's handling David's death, but she's not. Could you come back? And bring Alice, too. I think she needs to see the two of you alone, without the rest of the family." Bob listened for a moment, then said with relief, "Good. I'll see you soon."

Michael twisted the knob in time to hear Trish swearing a blue streak. It was so unlike her that he stopped, just inside the door. The swearing continued, broken up by deep sobs and an occasional slamming that sounded as if she were kicking the wall. Carefully, he walked around the corner. "Trish?"

She was leaning against the hall wall. Glancing back, she reached for a smile, failed, then kicked her bedroom door once more. "The damn thing's stuck again," she said, swiping at tears. "I've had about all I can take!"

"Here, relax, Dr. Michael will fix all." He shoved his shoulder against the door but it barely budged. "This really is stuck. How come you shut it from this side?"

"I was so mad I just pulled it shut behind me." Trish began to sound sheepish. "And then I kicked it and kicked it."

"Good solution."

"Are you making fun of me?"

"Heck, no. I'm agreeing with you. I always kick things when I'm angry. What are you angry about?"

"I'm not angry."

Trish was generally so sweet-tempered it amused Michael that she was being so stubborn. But he had to hide his smile. At least until she cooled off.

He slammed his shoulder against the door and it finally gave way.

"Thanks," Trish said, slipping past him.

"Don't shut it again for a while. Until my shoulder recovers."

Michael went into the kitchen, tossed his jacket over a chair, and rubbed his hands together. He felt good. It didn't matter that Trish was in a bad mood. Just being with her helped push his anxieties to the back of his mind.

Leaning over the refrigerator door, he made a sound of satisfaction. Trish had been to the store. He opened a Coke and drank half of it down. Then he pulled out the package of ground beef and wondered if Trish had anything special planned or if he should just make burgers. Michael was the first to admit he was no great cook, but as he'd told Trish on more than one occasion, "I'm eager." Letting that eagerness drive him now, he rolled up his sleeves and started to whistle.

Several minutes later Trish stood in the doorway between the kitchen and living room. Her face was scrubbed, all evidence of her tears washed away. The blond hair that framed her face was dark where the water had wet it. She looked beautiful and unspoiled.

"Sorry," she said.

"For what?" Michael was forming the hamburger into patties.

"For being upset. What are you doing?"

"Making dinner."

"Give me that. We're having tacos."

"Oh." Michael looked down at the hamburger

in his hands and for some reason Trish started to giggle.

"Didn't you see the taco shells?" she asked, pointing to the counter. They were right in front of him.

"No . . ."

"You're hopeless."

Realizing his ineptitude had helped ease her unhappiness, Michael was more than willing to let her take over. While she cooked, he sat on one of the rickety cafe chairs they'd purchased at a garage sale.

They had no table. Balancing paper plates on their laps, they tried to eat their tacos and carry on a conversation, but in the end they settled down to their favorite spot on the living room floor.

"I saw my mother today," Trish said, when she'd pushed her plate aside.

"Yeah?"

"We had a fight," she said soberly. "A terrible fight."

Michael looked at her, feeling her pain.

"She blames me for everything. She thinks"— Trish choked on the confession—"that I've tried to—to—seduce Jack."

"No."

Trish bobbed her head. "Yes, she does. She as much as said so. She thinks it's all my fault."

"No, Trish, listen." He scooted closer to her, touching her arm. "Your stepfather's a jerk. He's got real problems. She's got to know that."

"She doesn't." Trish was emphatic. "That's why she's been so unfriendly. She thinks I've tried to take him away from her."

"No way. You misunderstood her."

"She hates me," Trish whispered. "I could see it in her eyes."

Michael ground his teeth together. It was so unfair! Couldn't Jeri Clayton see Jack for the swine he was?

Prudently deciding now was not the time to bring up the fact that Jack Clayton had been asking about him, too, Michael gave her an affectionate squeeze. Just a quick one. Nothing that might frighten her.

He sighed. He was afraid for Trish. Afraid Jack Clayton wasn't going to ever leave her alone.

She sensed his anxiety. "Michael . . . ?"

"Don't worry, Trish," he said with a grimness far beyond his years. "Things'll work out. I'm gonna make sure of it."

Brooke heard the murmurs coming from upstairs. Dr. Horton and his wife had arrived a half an hour earlier and everyone was taking care of poor, tortured Julie.

Her shoulders slumped. It didn't matter. She couldn't work up any animosity toward her rival. It was too late. David was gone. She and Julie had both lost.

Never had Brooke felt so afraid and lonely. Always before she'd been able to pick herself up, dust herself off, and get on with her life—such as it was. But now, without David she had no life worth living. She had nothing.

She lay her head back on the couch staring at the sloped ceiling, trying to visualize David. All she could remember was the way he'd looked at Julie. He'd loved Julie. She'd seen it. And she'd tried to drag him away from her.

He's dead because of me.

A tear slipped down her cheek to land on the brocade sofa. She was hollow inside. There was no Brooke Hamilton left.

Slowly, she turned her cheek to the back of the sofa, squeezing her eyes closed. The tears eventually stopped coming but the emptiness was still there, an aching nothingness that represented her whole life.

She lifted her lids. Directly in her line of vision was Dr. Horton's black bag, sitting on the entry hall sideboard. It was open.

Brooke stared at it for several seconds, uncomprehendingly. Then her mind began to work, slowly at first, then ever faster.

She raised her head. Everyone was still upstairs. Standing up, she quietly crossed to the hall and listened at the bottom step.

"I think she'll be all right now," Tom Horton was saying. "She'll sleep for a few hours."

"Should I call you when she wakes up?" Bob asked.

"Oh, yes," Alice Horton cut in. "Please. Or do you think we should stay?"

Brooke stepped away from the stairway. She didn't have much time. Palms sweating, she looked in the doctor's bag and saw a variety of pills. Confused, she grabbed several vials. It didn't matter what they were, she reasoned. Enough of them would do the trick.

Footsteps sounded on the stairs. Brooke clutched the vials to her breast and slid out of sight, around the back of the staircase. Crossing her fingers that Dr. Horton wouldn't notice the missing pills yet, she held her breath.

"I've got a couple of calls to make," Tom said

as he opened the front door. "Then we'll come back."

The door shut behind them and Brooke heard Bob walk toward the den. Quickly she mounted the stairs, standing on the upper landing for several seconds in mute indecision before her eyes fell on David's door.

David's room.

She locked the bedroom door behind her, then went straight to the adjoining bathroom. There she set the vials on the counter. Little blue pills, round white pills, and red and white capsules.

Which to take?

Frustrated, Brooke thought hard, then realized there was one quick way to find out. Her steps cushioned by the thick carpet, she silently moved down the hall to Julie's bedroom. The door was ajar.

Brooke peeked inside. Julie lay sound asleep on the bed, her breathing deep and even. Casting an eye around the room, Brooke spied the sedatives on Julie's dresser. Red and white capsules. Perfect. They were the same stuff she had.

As quietly as she'd entered, Brooke glided out. Relocking David's bedroom door behind her, she went to the bathroom, grabbed up the pills, and shook out the entire vial. Her palm was full.

She turned on the water and filled a glass. Holding the glass in her other hand she took them two at a time, looking at herself in the mirror every few seconds. When she'd taken the lot she smiled at her reflection.

I'll be with you soon, David.

* * *

The tentative knock on Neil's office door nearly stopped his heart. Scolding himself for being so jumpy, he tried to stay still, hoping the intruder would just go away.

"Neil?" Amanda's voice sounded tremulously through the panels. "Are you in there? Roxie said you're not in, but I saw your car . . ."

Damn. Neil grimaced. *Not today.* She rattled the knob and Neil ground his teeth together. Then his long-buried sense of decency surfaced. "Just a minute, Amanda," he said tiredly. "I'll be right there."

In his own way he really cared about Amanda, but he just didn't have time for her right now. He knew she was scared. He even knew that if he gave her any indication that he was interested, she would marry him in an instant. She didn't want to be alone and she believed she loved him. Maybe she did. He just didn't know how he felt about her.

And he had too many problems of his own to give it much thought now.

"Oh, Neil." She tumbled into his arms. "I know you wanted a few days to yourself but I couldn't stand being without you."

Easing her down into one of the chairs, he said, "It's just that I've got some business to take care of. I told you that."

"Couldn't I just be with you?"

"Not right now. I've got to go out." The cashier's check was burning a hole in his pocket. He had to get to the bank.

"How about if I wait for you to come back?" she asked in a small voice.

"Amanda . . ." Neil was frustrated. He felt such dire urgency. "Look, I'll stop by your house as soon as I'm finished. Okay? We'll spend the night together."

"Could we stay at your house?"

"Sure. Anything you like."

"I'll meet you there at seven," Amanda said with relief.

"Seven." Neil tried to hustle her out of his office.

She rose and tugged on her gloves. With a rustle of silk, she headed for the door, giving Neil a whiff of expensive perfume as she passed. Amanda was made of money, there was no doubt about that.

"Seven," she said softly, almost shyly, then gave him a quick peck on the cheek.

Neil waited for her to leave. His hand went into his pocket. The envelope was still there. He waved and gave her a wink, his mind already churning. It seemed such a shame to take all that money and just put it in the office account. If he just had half of it to put down at Saturday night's game he could make a small fortune. No more money problems. He'd be on a par with Amanda Howard's income bracket—like he'd been before.

But the office needed the money.

Neil waited several minutes, then he went out the back door—only to find Greg Peters talking to Amanda. The young doctor's eyes were all over her and he was saying, " . . . I play tennis now and again at the Salem Racquet Club. How long have you been a member?"

"My—husband belonged," Amanda answered somewhat stiltedly.

"But you do play, don't you? If not, I know a great teacher . . ."

Before Neil had time to wipe the leer off Greg's face Amanda looked up and saw him. Her face cleared and Neil's jealousy vanished. She was still his.

But Greg gave him a cold look. "Neil," he said, with a short nod.

"Hello, Greg. Amanda."

"I'm glad you're here," Greg went on. "I've been trying to reach you for days."

"Look, Greg, this isn't the time."

"When is, then?"

"Soon."

"Is that your kind of soon, or my kind of soon?"

Greg's needling normally only irritated Neil, but this time he began to feel nervous. He had to fight not to loosen his collar. The last thing he needed was an upstart like Greg souring everything between himself and Amanda. He needed her to think he was as solvent as he'd ever been. It would be too galling to admit the real state of his finances. "I've got some calls to make, but I'll be back this afternoon."

Greg slid a knowing look in Amanda's direction. "You're sure."

"Of course I'm sure. I'll see you later."

Neil tore out of the lot. His moment of unease had vanished and now he was infuriated. Greg was like a broken record.

Resolving to end his partnership with the man, he waited at the corner until Amanda's car passed, going the other way. He didn't like her talking to Greg. He sensed, without really analyzing why, that to lose her would be to lose everything.

I'll never let Peters have her, he thought

viciously as he eased the Mercedes into traffic.

The line to the bank's drive-through window was long and he impatiently drummed his fingers on the steering wheel, the wheels in his mind turning. Half of the money was all he needed. Half would do nicely. A tidy sum, and Amanda Howard, too. How could he lose?

The cars slowly moved forward.

Actually, all the money would be that much better. The sky was the limit. Instead of writing IOU's to those other poker players, they'd be writing them to him.

At the last minute Neil pulled his car out of the line. He drove home. He would call Andy and tell him he was in for big stakes. He had a feeling this was it.

Lost in thought, Neil drove through the gathering twilight and pulled into his darkened garage. He cut the engine and stepped out. All he had to do was double his ante and—

Something hit him square in the chest, flattening him to the car. His breath came out in an "oof," and Neil scrambled to get up. Hard hands slammed him backward.

"Hello, Doc," Jimmy Sentra's familiar nasal tones sounded in the darkness. "We've been waitin' for ya."

Neil could only make out shapes, but he sensed there were at least three people in the garage—Sentra and a couple of his goons. A chill settled in his stomach. He tried to speak but a hand squeezed his throat, closing his windpipe.

"You ain't been delivering, Doc. Can't trust a man who won't keep his promises."

"Jimmy," Neil croaked hoarsely. The hand

around his throat eased a bit and he coughed several times. He'd never been so afraid. "I've got a cashier's check in my pocket. Just for you. All for you. I was just going in to call you."

"Sure ya were."

"Really. I'm telling the truth. It's in my right-hand pocket."

"Okay, boys." There was steel beneath the words. "It's time to teach the doc a lesson."

"No! I—"

Pain exploded in Neil's head. Bright lights spiraled behind his eyes. He slumped but no one caught him. Landing in a heap on the cold cement floor, he felt a boot kick his ribs, then another, and another, until he lost count.

He wasn't certain how long he lay there before Sentra grabbed him by the hair. "Time's up, Doc," he said. "That's all."

"The check," Neil mumbled, through slack lips. "Take the check."

Pain throbbed inside his skull but Neil desperately tried to hold on to his senses. The cashier's check was all he had left to save him.

"Check his pockets," Sentra instructed. "Just to make sure."

With relief, Neil felt hands roll him over, searching. The envelope rustled. There was a brief moment of silence, then Sentra said, "Well, well, well. You were tellin' the truth. But this is just a down payment. You're a long way from even. Stand him up, boys. He needs to endorse this."

Neil was unceremoniously jerked to his feet. His head whirled. A pen was placed in his right hand and the check was set on the roof of his car. His hand shook so badly he could barely write, but he managed to scratch out his name.

Thank God I had the money.

"Just so you won't forget me," Jimmy said, and Neil felt a bone-cracking blow to his ribs. The goons dropped him and he slid to the floor. He heard them walking away.

"The rest at the end of the week, Doc," Jimmy added. "My patience won't last no longer."

Neil lay quiet and still. He tasted blood. With what seemed to take hours, he slowly moved his head, feeling instant nausea. *Amanda*, he thought, swallowing hard. *Please hurry.*

His thoughts were drifting; he was barely aware of where he was. The sound of an engine brought him to full wakefulness and through the open garage he heard her unlatch her door, saw light spill from the interior of her car.

"Amanda," he whispered hoarsely.

She was walking toward the front door. She rang the bell several times and Neil tried to raise his head. Her returning footsteps were slower, and she stopped several times, as if trying to figure things out.

"Amanda," he managed a bit louder.

"Neil?"

He didn't have the strength to respond. All he could think about was falling into her arms.

"Neil?" Amanda tentatively stepped into the garage.

"Here . . ."

She walked quickly. From his vantage point he could see her white heels, her silky legs. "Oh, Neil," she breathed, distressed. Soft fingers touched his forehead, his temple. "What happened? Oh, my God. I've got to get you to the hospital!"

That seared through his brain. "No!"

"But you're hurt! What happened?" She sucked in her breath. "Who did this to you?"

"No one. Really. Amanda . . . please . . . help . . ."

He struggled to get to his feet and she asked anxiously, "Are you sure you should get up? Let me call an ambulance."

"*No*. I'm okay. Just help me."

Her arm slipped under his, supporting him. It took all Neil's strength, and Amanda's, but they managed to get him into the house. His footsteps were heavy and each one cost dearly, but he made it to the couch. Amanda knelt beside him.

"Darling, you look terrible," she worried. "Let me get a washcloth."

"Water . . . please."

She hurried away and Neil lay completely still, waiting for his head to clear. He hurt all over, but knew that apart from a cracked rib or two, he was basically okay. He could bandage his chest himself. What he couldn't do, was let it get out that he'd been roughed up by Jimmy Sentra.

Amanda came back with a glass of ice water and a warm rag. She dabbed at his forehead and Neil flinched. He was going to have to take a few days off, he realized, until the worst of his injuries disappeared. Otherwise Greg would start with the questions again.

"What happened?" Amanda asked.

"It was an old vendetta," Neil said, knowing he couldn't completely lie to Amanda. She'd seen too much. But he could bend the truth a little. "Over a long-ago love affair."

She stared down at him. "What do you mean?"

"I was seeing this woman who was separated from her husband but he, well, he thought he had ownership rights. Ouch! Amanda, let up!"

"Another woman?" She looked ready to cry. "Be honest with me, Neil."

"Look, my love. It was all a long time ago. You're the only woman in my life now. And that's the truth." Neil looked at her loveliness, thought about her wealth, wondered what it was that had kept him from making a commitment in the past, and asked, "Would you marry me?" before his courage deserted him.

Amanda blinked. "Marry—you?"

"Yes." The word nearly stuck in his throat. He didn't want to get married; he wanted her money. The small, decent part of him that was still alive cried out against this travesty.

But Amanda's eyes were shining. "Oh, Neil! Yes, yes, yes! I was afraid you'd never get around to asking! When? When do you want to get married?"

He tried to smile and failed. "As soon as possible."

Tears slid down her cheeks. "I'll make you so happy. I promise. I love you so much, Neil."

"I love you, too, Amanda."

And he wished, with true fervor, that it could be so.

The doorbell went through its melodious peals and Bob twisted the knob long before the last note sounded.

"Hello, again," Tom said, shaking Bob's hand. "How's everything going?"

"Julie's still sleeping," he said, taking both

Tom and Alice's coats. "I just checked on her."

"Good."

"Should we wait until she awakens?" Alice
wondered.

Bob led the way into the living room. "I would
like you both to stay," he admitted. "I hardly
know what to do."

Tom heaved a sigh. "Only time will heal her
now."

Brooke's tattered coat was spread over the
back of the sofa. Bob picked it up and was half-
way to the hall closet when it occurred to him
that she'd been noticeably absent for the last
couple hours. He couldn't recall seeing her since
before Julie had taken her sedative.

"Did you see Brooke outside when you got
back?" he asked, walking back to the living
room.

Tom and Alice shook their heads.

Feeling uneasy, Bob turned on the backyard
lights and looked out the window. Rain dripped
unevenly from the overflowing eaves, but there
was no sign of Brooke. "That's funny," he murmured.

"Maybe she went upstairs to take a nap,"
Alice suggested.

It made perfect sense but Bob couldn't shake
his uneasiness. *You're letting the day get to you*,
he told himself.

Tom Horton hadn't acheived a reputation as
one of Salem's best doctors on skill alone. Now
he picked up on Bob's anxiety. "You think
something's wrong?"

"I don't know. No. Probably not." He
shrugged, looking over his shoulder. "Brooke
was just so upset . . ."

"Maybe you should check on her."

It was hardly his place to do so. Brooke was a houseguest, little more than an acquaintance really, and she'd shown how she valued her independence on more than one occasion. But Bob felt a responsibility he couldn't ignore. "I'll be right back," he said, heading for the stairway.

The house was incredibly quiet as he hurried up the thickly carpeted steps. So quiet, in fact, that Bob could hear the sound of his own heartbeats. He ducked his head in Julie's bedroom first, making certain she was all right. Her breathing was even, restful. Reassured, he went down the hall to Brooke's room and tapped softly on her door.

"Brooke?"

No answer. Twisting the knob, Bob peeked his head inside. The room was empty, as was the adjoining bathroom. Every bedroom in the house Bob had designed for his new bride had a bathroom, and as he stood in the center of the room, perplexed, he thought he heard water running in the bathroom on the other side of the wall. David's bathroom.

A cold chill skittered down his spine.

Quickly he ran down the hall, turning the handle to David's room. The door was locked.

"Tom!" he yelled at the top of his lungs.

He heard the older man come running at his call, but he didn't wait. He slammed his shoulder into the door. It groaned but didn't break. He kicked at the lock. Wood splintered.

Tom rounded the first landing. "She's locked herself in," he said, his grim voice an echo of Bob's own sentiments.

For an answer Bob slammed his shoulder into the door again and this time it gave way. He heard the water and turned toward the bathroom but then he saw Brooke and his breath caught.

She was lying on David's bed, completely clothed, even her shoes were still on. Her eyes were closed but she was so still. Too still.

Bob's muscles slackened. *She's dead*, he thought hopelessly.

Then Tom was in the room, checking her pulse, her pupils. "Call an ambulance," he ordered. "Now!"

Bob tried to move but nothing happened.

"For God's sake get a grip on yourself!" Tom jerked his head around. "If you can't handle it, get Alice to! *Just do it! Now.*"

Bob fled from the room and ran to the telephone. "This is an emergency," he said to the operator. "I need an ambulance right away . . ."

Chapter Eight
Looking for Love

Tom Horton walked down the empty hallways of the hospital and checked the clock. Midnight. He grimaced and wiped his brow. It had taken a long time and he'd begun to think Brooke Hamilton wouldn't make it. But luck had been with her—and with them. Now she was resting peacefully.

There was no one in the waiting room. Poignantly, he wondered if anyone really cared whether Brooke lived or died. Because he was her one connection, Tom phoned Bob, glad somehow to find he was still awake and waiting for news.

"She's going to be all right. We pumped her stomach but she'd taken a lot of pills and the drug was in her bloodstream. Luckily, she hadn't completely overdosed before we got to her."

"Thank God," Bob said fervently.

Tom felt sympathy for him. This ordeal hadn't been easy on any of them but Bob had had to be stalwart and strong for both Julie and

Brooke. And Bob had never impressed Tom as a particularly strong man himself.

"Does she have any family we could contact?"

"I really don't know," Bob admitted on a heavy sigh. "She was just David's girlfriend, if you know what I mean."

Just David's girlfriend. Tom understood only too well. He hoped somewhere there was someone who loved her. "She's out of danger but that doesn't mean she'll be happy when she awakens. She's hurting, Bob. Just like Julie is."

"I'll try to come see her tomorrow," Bob said vaguely. "Good-bye, Tom. And thanks."

Hanging up, Tom tried to shake off his feeling of defeat. He'd saved a life. He should be glad. Instead he had a terrible premonition that he'd just prolonged Brooke Hamilton's anguish.

Amanda held up the street-length cream silk dress for Neil's inspection. "Isn't it gorgeous? I thought about velvet. Maybe even full-length, but I haven't been a widow all that long. It didn't seem quite right."

Neil managed a smile. His face was tight with the effort, but felt better than it had. Almost normal. The swelling had gone down and he was left with a few bruises and a black eye. Maybe he'd be able to get past Greg without a lot of unnecessary questions if he went to work. Anything would be better than living out this fantasy with Amanda.

Why had he ever asked her to marry him?

The question was rhetorical and answered as instantly as he'd posed it: Jimmy Sentra. The only reason Neil was still in one piece was because he'd leaked the information of his pending marriage.

With Amanda's money on the horizon, Sentra had agreed to give him a little more time.

"Or do you like this better?" Amanda asked, pulling a pale peach gown of some shimmery fabric from the depths of her huge bedroom closet. "It's more dressy. Maybe too much for a wedding. What do you think?"

"I like them both."

She glanced from one dress to the other. "I don't know. I really liked that velvet gown. Maybe I should go back and get it."

Neil didn't want to think about how much money Amanda was discussing; it made him feel slightly sick. Money. That's what had caused all his present-day problems. If only Sentra had let him keep the cashier's check. He could be rich by now!

Instead, he was facing imminent matrimony.

He got up stiffly, favoring his ribs. Fleetingly, he toyed with the idea of asking Amanda for some front money. One big score and he'd be back on top of the world. But he looked at her face and knew he couldn't spoil her happiness. With a sigh, he walked to the huge bay window at the far corner of the bedroom suite.

"Neil?"

"I'm fine, sweetheart. Just a few aches and pains left, that's all."

"You're not getting second thoughts on me, are you?" she teased, coming up behind him and slipping her arms tenderly around him.

"Of course not."

"I need you so much, Neil," she said, resting her cheek on his back. "Don't ever leave me. Promise?"

The view from Amanda's window was exquisite. Far to the left, the slow waters of the river curved around a bend, free and serene. Neil watched them flow by for a long moment.

"Promise," he said.

Bob rubbed his jaw, struggling with indecision. He stood on the upper landing, his gaze turning from Julie's door to Brooke's and back again. He wasn't sure he'd done the right thing by offering his home to Brooke again. Letting her stay at his house might just aggravate Julie's grief. Yet, what choice did he have? Throw her out in the street? He knew so little about her.

When Tom had brought Brooke home from the hospital, Bob had been ready to tell her he'd take her anywhere she wanted to go but that she had to leave. His initial desire to help had dissipated; he already had one grieving woman to take care of.

But one look at her pinched cheeks and white face had changed his mind—at least for the time being. He hadn't had the heart to turn her away.

So now he was right back where he'd started.

He glanced to her doorway again, then slowly headed downstairs. "When she wakes up I'll send her home," he muttered. "Taking care of Julie is enough."

The sound of her husband's car pulling into the drive brought Susan to her feet. Quickly, she lit the candles on the table, then blew out the match and cast one last look around the room. Perfect. Soft music drifted from the stereo, a bouquet of fresh scarlet and tangerine flowers stood on the table, the crystal shimmered under the chandelier.

She smoothed the skirt of her black dress. The fabric was sheer, almost see-through. With a smile flirting around the corners of her mouth, she arranged herself on one of the chairs. Greg wasn't going to know what hit him.

The car door slammed, she heard a jingle of keys, footsteps, then Greg came through the back door and stopped dead.

"Hi," Susan said.

"What's all this?" Frowning, he tossed his briefcase on the sofa and loosened his tie.

"What does it look like?"

"I'd be afraid to ask."

Anger slid through her but Susan controlled it. Now was not the time to blow up. "I wanted tonight to be special."

"Look, I'm really tired. It's not the best time for romance, Susan. I'm sorry."

He walked out of the room and down the hallway.

She stared after him in disbelief. What kind of woman did he think she was? "Greg! Come back here right now!"

There was no answer.

Enraged, she ran after him, stopping just inside the bedroom doorway, shaking, while she watched him undress. He ignored her and headed for the shower.

Susan followed. "You were with her tonight, weren't you?" she accused.

The water came on, effectively drowning her out. Infuriated beyond reason, Susan unsnapped the shower door, reached in, and turned off the taps.

"Hey—"

"You're not leaving me, Greg. I won't let you."

"Shut the door," he said irritably, turning on the spray.

"Damn you, Greg!"

"Your timing is wrong. That's all." He grabbed the door and tried to shut it, but she struggled with him. Her hands lost their grip on the wet glass and the door slammed shut with a resounding snap.

"You can lie all you want but it won't help!" she shouted.

Greg swore under his breath.

"I know you're seeing someone else. I can feel it. I won't let you have her. I won't!"

When there was no answer she stalked back to the dining room. Her fury consumed her. She wanted to kill him!

She grabbed the candles and doused them under the kitchen taps. "One of these days, Greg, you'll push me too far." Her face was set. "One of these days."

Bob twisted to look at the clock, the phone cord wrapped around him. He was late getting to work. "Harry, I'll be there by eleven at the latest," he said. "Tell the electrician to wait. Pay him in advance, if you have to. But just get him to stay until I can get there."

"Okay." Bob's foreman sounded dubious.

"It's just these damn family crises," Bob said with feeling. "I'll be there."

He'd barely hung up when the doorbell rang. Good Lord, what now? Muttering under his breath, he glanced toward the stairway. Julie was at least up and about and looking better, but the situation was far from normal yet. He couldn't depend on her for anything.

And Brooke had been a walking zombie since she'd returned. Bob wasn't certain he could cope with her much longer. He wished she'd just snap out of it so they could all get on with their lives.

"Certified letter for Mr. Robert Anderson," the postman said, handing Bob a pen. "Sign here."

Bob scratched out his name, glancing at the letter curiously. It was from an attorney and postmarked Ash Grove. Mystified, he turned it over in his hands. Ash Grove? He couldn't imagine who it was from.

He shut the door and walked into the den. Sliding open the seal with his letter opener, Bob pulled out a single typewritten sheet and a sealed lavender envelope. He read the letter quickly and was shocked. It was about Adele! On her solicitor's letterhead it matter-of-factly explained how she'd died the week before from cirrhosis of the liver. She'd wanted Bob to have the sealed envelope upon the event of her death.

Memories filled him as Bob opened the envelope and pulled out a single handwritten page on faded lavender stationery. He'd nearly forgotten about Adele. It had been a long time ago. Wondering what she could possibly have wanted to say to him, Bob checked the date on the letter. It was nearly ten years earlier. An uneasiness settled in him.

Dearest Bob, Though years have passed I've never stopped loving you . . .

Adele Hamilton. He smiled sadly and shook his head. Their affair had been brief and fiery. Adele Hamilton. Hamilton? His memory jogged. The same last name as Brooke's?

. . . I've kept a secret from you only because I

*didn't want to spoil your marriage to Phyllis. We
have a daughter, Bob. A beautiful girl I've
named Brooke.*

Bob's jaw slackened. The words blurred in
front of his eyes. He had to fight to read on.

*I cannot truly believe we won't see each other
again, but in case we don't, I wanted you to
know the truth. Brooke is your daughter, Bob.
Yours and mine. Please find her and take care
of her. Love forever, Adele.*

"Bob?"

He started violently, crumpling the paper in
his hand. Julie was standing in the doorway.
"Well . . . hello . . ." He shoved the letter in his
pocket and tried to act naturally.

But Julie had seen his actions. "Is something
wrong?"

"No."

"You put something in your pocket. A paper."

"Oh, that . . ." Bob's mind raced. He couldn't
tell Julie about Brooke. Not now. He couldn't
believe it himself. "It was a letter from, er, one
of my subs. Looks like he's in bankruptcy. He's
skipped town before the job's done and the cred-
itors want full payment from me."

"Oh." She lost interest and turned away. "I
was going to make some toast and coffee. Want
some?"

"No thanks. I've got to get to work. You
might ask Brooke," he tentatively suggested.

"Brooke left."

"Left?"

"She took off in David's car early this morning. I saw her go. I hope she never comes
back."

Julie turned toward the kitchen. Bob stared

blankly after her. Brooke couldn't leave! Not
now! He had to find her.

But he had to get to work, too.

Clenching his jaw, Bob banked down his
urgency to see Brooke—his daughter!—and
headed for the construction site. She'd be back.
She had nowhere else to go anyway. Her
mother was dead. Resolving to call the solicitors
just in case Brooke made a trip to Ash Grove,
Bob let the news fully sink in.

He had two daughters. Mary and Brooke.
And Julie was pregnant. It was overwhelming,
but it made him feel good. Being responsible for
Brooke had suddenly taken on a new dimension.
He was her father!

He couldn't wait to tell her.

The beat-up Ford was on its last legs. It
wheezed and rattled into the parking lot behind
Doug's Place. Brooke cut the engine and waited
for it to cool, feeling absurdly close to tears.
This was David's car. All she had left of him.

Why hadn't they just let her die?

Slamming the door, she walked through the
frigid night, oblivious to the cold. She'd been to
several bars already and had drunk enough to
keep her warm. But her mind was ice clear.
She needed something besides alcohol to
deaden the pain.

Doug's Place was warm and filled with noise
and laughter. It made Brooke feel better. She
thought of the bartender she'd turned down several weeks earlier and wondered if he was on
duty this evening. For some reason, she thought
of him as a friend.

The man mixing drinks was a stranger.

Brooke sat on one of the bar stools and ordered a rum and Coke. Sipping it, she morosely considered the ruins of her life and wondered if there was any point in salvaging it. The issue would be moot if Bob and Dr. Horton hadn't reached her when they did. She wondered if they knew how much she resented their valiant lifesaving efforts.

"Hello, gorgeous."

Brooke ignored the admiring male voice. He had to be talking to someone else. *She* wasn't gorgeous. It was too much trouble to be gorgeous. Her hair hadn't seen a comb in weeks, and she couldn't even remember what she was wearing without taking a look.

The bar stool next to her creaked with the weight of another body. "Not interested in conversation, huh?" the voice asked again.

Brooke slid him a disinterested glance from the corner of her eye. He was tall, with dark hair long enough to brush the back of his collar. His eyes were blue and his smile was full of the devil.

He looked a lot like David.

She glanced down at her clothes. Jeans and a rumpled blouse. Licking her lips, Brooke suddenly wished she'd taken more care with her appearance, put on some makeup. She tried to think up some clever response but for once, words failed her. She smiled faintly.

Encouraged, the man scooted his stool closer. "Could I buy you another one of those?" He pointed to her half-full glass.

"Sure."

"My name's Ted," he said. "What's yours?"

"Brooke."

"Brooke," he repeated thoughtfully. "That's a pretty name."

"Where are you from?" asked Brooke. If she closed her eyes just so, and didn't think about his voice . . .

"Salem. You?"

"No. I grew up in Ash Grove. A little town north of here." Brooke took a heavier swallow. The guy could be David's twin.

"Want to dance?"

She nodded and let Ted take her hand. His skin felt cool and dry, just like David's. She let him pull her close, tight against him. The rhythm of his body struck a distant chord. David. She remembered lying next to him, making love to him.

Ted's lips were searching her hair. "Mmmm," he growled low in his throat, "you smell good."

Tilting her chin, Brooke gave him access to her lips. His mouth was eager. She liked his kisses.

"It's really getting hot in here," he murmured. "Why don't we move this party to my hotel? I've got some cool drinks ready and waiting in my room."

"Anything you say, David."

"Great." He pulled her toward the door. "It's Ted, honey."

Brooke's eyes were slumbrous. It only took a little imagination. "That's what I said," she murmured softly and they walked into the clear fall night.

"Brooke hasn't come back yet," Bob said worriedly. He cut into his lamb chop and forced a piece into his mouth, chewing without tasting.

"Do you care?" Julie listlessly pushed her vegetables around on her plate, then set down her fork.

"Well, yeah. I don't want anything to happen to her. David's death has been hard on her, too."

Silent tears began to slide down Julie's cheeks. Seeing them, Bob couldn't help but feel impatient. Would things ever get back to normal?

The phone rang, startling them both. "I'll get it," Bob said, and hurriedly left. Maybe it was Brooke, checking in.

"Hello, Dad?"

For a moment Bob was thunderstruck, thinking it was Brooke. But then he realized it was Mary. "Well, hello, sweetheart," he said, disappointed.

"I hadn't talked to you in a while and I got kinda worried. How's Julie?"

"Fine. Better, anyway." Bob didn't elaborate. There had never been any love lost between his daughter and his wife; Mary couldn't forgive Julie for, as she saw it, stealing Bob away from her mother, Phyllis.

"When are you stopping by? Mother says she hasn't seen you in weeks."

"I've been busy, honey. I'll get around there soon."

"You're not forgetting about me just because you're about to become a new father, are you?" Mary asked lightly.

"Of course not." *If she only knew*, he thought, uncomfortably reminded of Brooke.

"Then when can I see you?" she pressed. "Sometimes it seems like I don't even have a father anymore."

"What about Saturday? Or Sunday. Weekends are best for me, you know that."

"Sunday evening. Here. I'll make dinner for you, me, and Mom."

"I'll try, but I can't make any promises. Besides, your mother might have made other plans."

"No she hasn't. I asked her."

"Well, things are just really unsettled around here, Mary. Let me get back to you."

"Oh, sure. Great." Mary sniffed. "You call me when you can make the time. But don't put yourself out."

The phone went dead before Bob had a chance to respond. He hung up, waiting for the anger he was sure would follow. Instead he felt relief. One less problem to contend with. He could make up to Mary and Phyllis later—for now he had other problems, and his biggest one was finding Brooke.

The skies were beginning to darken but the air was crisp and clean as Michael collected his earnings from Lou, stuck his hands in his pockets, hiked up his backpack, and began trekking to his apartment. He didn't have to work the next morning if he didn't want to, and in this case, he didn't want to. It was Friday night and he felt like partying.

An hour later, he crossed the broken asphalt parking lot that led to his apartment, glad to see lights on. Trish was home.

"I'm back," he called, slinging his pack on the kitchen counter. "Hey, something smells great."

"I'm experimenting," Trish's voice came from down the hall. A couple minutes later she appeared, her hair clipped loosely into a blond knot on the top of her head. "It's chicken in wine," she said, grinning. "My friend gave me the recipe."

"Who gave you the wine?"

"I just walked in the store and bought it." Trish tilted up her chin.

"Wow." Michael grinned and whistled appreciatively.

"Double wow. I bought some champagne, too."

"What's the occasion?" He was trying hard not to stare too hard at her, but she looked so sweet and beguiling in a soft pink V-necked sweater that showed off her figure in ways Michael would have just as soon forgotten.

"No occasion, really. The opportunity just presented itself and I grabbed it." She leaned on her tiptoes and gave him a self-conscious peck on the cheek. "You've been so good to me."

Her breast touched his arm and it felt like a jolt of electricity. Michael swallowed. "Want me to open the champagne?"

"Do it." She smiled up at him, her blue eyes crinkling at the corners. "I'll fix dinner."

With the help of his small task, and the pop of the cork followed by a bubbling froth over his hands, Michael was able to put his feelings for Trish aside for the moment. It wouldn't do to think about her that way, too much. She was a friend. Period.

As she worked on the meal, chatting continually about her new job and friends, Michael listened in silence, trying to concentrate on what she was saying. It was no easy task. Just looking at her was enough to send his hormones into fits.

They sat cross-legged on the living room floor. He told her the chicken was out of this world when in reality he barely tasted it. When Trish moved, even to take a bite, he saw different curves and angles of her body. To cool his ardor he turned his eyes away, but his memory refused to dissolve. It was achingly clear. Disruptive.

"More champagne?" she asked, leaning forward to fill his plastic cup.

Michael's head was spinning. He could see down the front of her sweater to the dusky hollow between her breasts. "Thanks," he said with an effort.

"I feel great." Trish sighed, lying back on the floor, a pillow propped beneath her head. She was inches away from him. "So relaxed." She giggled. "I think we should drink champagne every night."

"Good idea."

"I can even think about Jack without getting all tensed up. You know, for the longest time I hated being in the house when he was there. I couldn't even sleep. I kept thinking he might creep into my room one night." She shuddered. "Ugh. But then you came and rescued me."

"That's me." Michael carefully lay his head back, stretched out beside her. "A knight in shining armor."

Trish sighed. "I almost feel sorry for Jack. I *do* feel sorry for my mother."

"Don't feel sorry for Jack." Michael struggled to enunciate clearly. "He stopped by the garage the other day, asking Lou about me."

"He did?"

"Uh-huh. I didn't want to say anything because I thought it might scare you."

Trish propped herself up on one elbow, leaning over him. "It does, a little," she admitted. "But I'm not going to let it."

Her scent hung over him like a sweet cloud. Michael closed his eyes. "Oh, Trish," he moaned. Though he knew it was all wrong, he reached up to give her a comforting hug.

He didn't intend for anything to happen. Just one hug. That's all. But then his eyes opened and he saw into the pure depths of hers.

"I keep hoping the problem will just go away," she whispered.

"Me, too." His arms were around her but she wasn't alarmed. Just trusting and innocent, needing him to reassure her. He licked his lips. "Jack'll smarten up sometime," he promised.

His body was a traitor; his arms tightened of their own accord.

"Michael . . ." Trish said protestingly. He'd pulled her half on top of him.

He swallowed. Later he would bitterly chastise himself for what happened next. But at that moment, with champagne clouding his judgment and her body touching his, Michael just reacted. He slid his hand around her head and brought her lips down to his and kissed her, her mouth soft and trembling.

"Michael!"

"Don't, Trish," he murmured, tightening his hold.

"Let go of me!"

"No . . . please, it's all right."

Her panic was instantaneous. She fought like a wild woman. Michael held on until his wits returned, then he dropped his arms, sick with himself. She was up in a flash, running, tripping over her shoes. Michael tried to rise and stumbled, swearing as he fell on the couch. "Trish! I'm sorry!" he called, but the door to her bedroom slammed shut.

"Trish . . ." He rolled clumsily to his feet. Remorse ate through the champagne euphoria. Knocking softly on her door, he said, "Oh, Trish, I'm really sorry. I didn't mean to kiss you. It just seemed right." He jiggled the knob. "Trish? Can you hear me?"

For an answer he heard muffled sobs. She was crying into her pillow.

Aching, Michael leaned his head on the wall. He felt close to tears himself; they burned behind his eyes. *You stupid, stupid idiot! What the hell did you think you were doing?*

Pushing himself away from the wall he staggered outside, gulping in air. His head ached and he felt like throwing up. "You stupid, stupid bastard!" he choked.

He'd just lost the only true friend he had.

Chapter Nine

The Dark Before The Dawn

A country and western classic crooned from the radio of the silver pickup and its driver hummed along with it, drumming one palm on the dashboard. Michael just looked out the window, hoping he'd be dropped somewhere near the center of town.

"You like C and W, boy?" the driver asked, pushing back his Stetson.

"It's okay."

"It's more'n okay. It's all there is."

Michael wasn't about to argue the point. As long as the guy kept driving, he was satisfied to listen to whatever the cowboy desired.

The pickup turned onto the street that led into Salem and Michael's throat constricted. *Home*, he thought.

They drove to the business section of town and beyond, toward Salem General. Settling back in his seat, Michael wiped his palms on his jeans. He wasn't sure why he was so nervous. This was just a visit, after all, a chance to see his mother and talk to her.

"This okay, boy?" The driver pulled up to the curb, engine throbbing.

Unlatching the door, Michael climbed down from the cab. "Perfect."

"You said the hospital, didn't ya?"

"Yeah. Thanks."

"Not sick, are ya?"

"Nope. Somebody I know works here."

Michael waved as the silver pickup took off, then he dodged between cars on the main street, ignoring the blaring horns. The lobby of Salem General was fairly empty and he skirted the main reception area, not wanting anyone to recognize him.

Inside the elevator he wondered what he would do if his mother wasn't at work. He'd be damned if he would go find Bill. No, if worse came to worst, he'd go home, wait for her there, and pray that Bill was kept late at work.

Feeling eyes on him, Michael met the stare of a young intern. The intern's gaze slid away, but not before Michael had been given the once-over. Without having to look, he knew what the intern had seen: grease-shiny, ragged-cuffed jeans, faded T-shirt, worn jacket. Self-consciously, Michael shifted his weight from one foot to the other.

Outside his mother's office door the nameplate read: DR. LAURA HORTON, PSYCHIATRIST. Taking a deep breath, he walked inside.

The reception room was empty except for Peg, Laura's receptionist-cum-bookkeeper. Upon seeing Michael her lips parted and she looked toward the open inner-office door. Michael could hear his mother on the phone.

". . . I've just got to make a few more phone calls, Bill, and I'll meet you downstairs in the

lobby. There's this one patient who refuses to
see me. I know I should give up but it's so frus-
trating. Sometimes I can feel her reaching for
my help . . ."

Bill. Michael's mouth felt dry. The reasons
he'd left home came crashing back down on
him, burying him in unhappy memories.

But were they really so unhappy? Compared
to the mess he'd made of his new life, he wasn't
so sure.

"Fifteen minutes," Laura was saying. "I promise I won't be late. Scout's honor." She hung up
the phone and walked to the outer office, a file
in her hand. "Peg, I've put in another call to
Amanda Howard but I'm leaving a little early. If
you hear from her please—"

"Dr. Horton," Peg interrupted anxiously, gesturing in Michael's direction.

Laura turned. "Michael," she said, her breath
catching.

He suddenly had no idea what to say to her.
"Hi, Mom."

"What are you doing here? I thought you
weren't, well . . . I thought you didn't want to
come home," she finished weakly.

"Could I talk to you alone?"

It was all Laura could do to keep from scoop-
ing him into her arms. He looked so young and
forlorn, yet there was something different about
him—a new maturity—that made her keep her
distance. "Sure. Come in my office."

"I heard you tell Bill you'd be right down," he
said as she shut the door behind them.

"He'll understand."

"Will he?" Michael flopped into one of the
chairs.

"Yes." She smiled. "He will."

In her profession Laura had learned to let the patient lead, the doctor follow. Though she didn't understand why, she sensed that now she had to treat her son as a patient, waiting until he spelled out his reasons for coming home.

"I wanted to talk to you," he said, looking down at his hands. "I wanted to see you, and talk to you."

"About Bill?"

"No."

"About us? Our relationship?"

"It's nothing like that." Michael stood again and walked toward the windows. "I made a mistake and I don't know how to fix it."

"What kind of mistake?"

"I hurt somebody. Somebody I care about."

Laura was quiet. From the first joyous moment she'd seen him she'd naturally assumed he'd come home to her. But his tone suggested differently. He wasn't concerned with her and Bill. There was someone new in his life. Someone important. And he'd come to her only because she was a psychiatrist; being his mother was of secondary importance.

"How did you hurt this person?"

He snorted in self-deprecation. "Oh, Mom, I came on to her. And I shouldn't have. It just destroyed everything."

Laura cleared her throat, deciding mothers should not be allowed to counsel their own sons. "What do you mean by 'came on'?"

"Don't get panicky." Michael almost smiled at her careful tone. "It was nothing. I just kissed her. But to Trish it was like . . . like . . . an attack!"

"Trish?"

"My roommate. She's"—he searched his mind and couldn't come up with a better superlative— "terrific."

"But you're not romantically involved with her yet?" Laura asked, feeling her way.

"We haven't had sex, if that's what you're asking."

Laura sighed. "Yes, I guess that's what I'm asking. I'm sorry, Michael. I'm trying. It's just hard after—not seeing you and all."

"Yeah, I know."

There was a long silence. Realizing he'd been unfair to her, just expecting her to be there, welcoming with open arms, accepting whatever he threw at her, Michael lifted a palm. "Look, I know you have to meet Bill. I don't want to screw up your plans."

"Aren't you coming home, too?"

"I'd like to talk to you," Michael said, grimacing, "but I really don't want to face Bill. No offense."

Laura thought hard. "What if . . . what if I went down and told Bill the situation and then you and I went somewhere for a while, just the two of us . . . to talk?"

"You'd do that?"

"Oh, Michael. I'd do practically anything for you. I won't deny that it hurts, the way you feel about Bill. But, well . . . you're too important to me to just turn you away. I'll go tell Bill."

"Wait." Michael hesitated, looking at his mother. He knew how much she wanted him to like his stepfather. It was never going to happen as far as he was concerned, but he could at least be civil and make a stab at peace. "Maybe we could catch a ride with him. But I'd rather talk to you alone."

Her face lit up. "Great. No problem. Let's go. And I want to hear all about Trish."

Michael followed his mother down the hall to the elevator. She slipped her arms through her coat and said, "This Trish is really important to you, isn't she?"

"She's my whole life," he said simply. "But she hates me."

"Oh, I doubt that."

"You don't know the whole story."

Laura gave him a long look as the elevator doors clanged shut. "Then maybe you should tell me it."

Impulsively, Michael gave her a quick squeeze. Sometimes it ticked him off that his mother was always trying to psychoanalyze him, but for once he was grateful "That's why I'm here," he admitted. "And to see you, too, of course."

"Of course." Laura kept a straight face and Michael half-laughed.

"Okay, okay. Guilty as charged. I need help."

The doors opened and Laura touched her son's arm lightly. "I'm glad you came to me."

Bill was waiting near the glass revolving doors. A look of incredulity spread across his face, quickly replaced by joy. "Michael . . . ?"

Michael felt Laura tense beside him. He met his stepfather's eyes, saw the uncertainty lurking there, and knew what he had to do. Sticking out his hand, he said, "Hello, Bill. I came back to see my mom for a few days. I don't want to fight."

It was rare that Bill Horton was at a loss for words; he'd been known to argue a point into the ground. But he was at a loss now. He swallowed several times, needing to tell Michael that he was his father so much that the words strangled him. But he couldn't shake the tenuous olive branch his son had offered him. Accepting his hand, he said hoarsely, "Neither do I, Michael. Neither do I."

It felt as though someone were holding her eyelids down, Brooke thought, opening them with an effort. Her head throbbed and her tongue felt woolly. She squinted and saw the room was dark, the shades drawn. Where was she?

Her legs were tangled in a sheet and as she tried to extricate herself she realized she had nothing on. *Oh, that's right. David. I'm here with David.*

But the fantasy disintegrated as soon as she looked at the man lying next to her. It wasn't David. Not by a long shot. She rubbed her eyes and took a harder look. It wasn't even the man she'd picked up at Doug's Place!

Brooke lifted her head and felt a clanging ache. Inhaling, she wrinkled her nose at the smell of stale alcohol. How much had she had to drink?

Squeezing her eyes shut again, she tried to remember, but all she could recall were the terrible days of her youth. Adele drunk on the couch. Adele with another lover. Empty bottles. Spilled drinks. Smoldering cigarettes.

With a cry she threw off the covers, stumbled out of bed, and pulled the top sheet around her, weaving on her feet. *She wasn't like her mother!*

"Whas'a matter, hon?" the stranger mumbled, plucking at the bedclothes she'd disturbed. He lifted bloodshot eyes to hers.

Brooke was repulsed. "What time is it?"

"Don't know." He lay back down.

She saw her clothes strung across the room. Picking them up one by one, she put them on. The man's arm was dangling over the side of the bed and she saw he had on a cheap watch. Twisting it around she noted the time. Ten o'clock.

"Hey," he protested, groaning.

Where had she found this guy? She couldn't remember. The last thing she recalled was going home with the man from Doug's Place. The one who looked like David. Ted. That was his name. Ted. But this man wasn't Ted.

"What's your name?" she asked.

"Hugh," he grunted.

Brooke looked around the tiny room and shuddered. Quietly she let herself into the hall.

I'm not like my mother. I'm not.

She hurried away, feeling the ghosts of her past following after her, threatening to form her future. The hotel lobby was little more than a scarred counter. Letting herself out the dirt-grimed doors, she glanced this way and that. She was still in Salem; she could see familiar buildings silhouetted against the morning sky.

How long had she been gone?

She walked up to a newsstand, feeling uneasy. Looking at the morning paper, she stood in stupefaction. The date read Thursday, November 15th.

She'd gone to Doug's Place on Saturday night.

"I'm getting married in the morning," Amanda sang, grinning as she angled the cream silk hat over her head. She felt like hugging herself, she was so happy. "Ding, dong the bells are gonna chime . . ."

Humming the rest, she set the hat down and glanced around her bedroom. Tomorrow night, she and Neil would be here, as man and wife. Then the next day they were taking off for Europe. Neil hadn't really wanted to go, complaining of too much work, but she'd talked him into it. They both needed some R & R.

Amanda sighed and made a face at herself in the mirror. Greg Peters hadn't been exactly thrilled to find out Neil was taking off. In fact, when she'd blurted out the news Greg had gone so quiet she'd begun to feel anxious. What was it between Greg and Neil? For sharing medical offices, they certainly seemed to treat each other with unusual distance.

It was too bad, too. Amanda liked Greg. He struck her as sincere, hardworking, and genuine— the kind of man you could confide in. She also knew that he liked her. Maybe even more than he should, considering he was married.

A little like the pot calling the kettle black, isn't it? she berated herself, remembering her affair with Neil while Charles was still alive.

But that was all past history now. She was marrying Neil and she could think of Charles without falling apart or expecting him to appear from thin air. Her nightmares had even ceased. Her life was getting back on track.

"And it's about time," she said aloud, grinning at her reflection.

A sharp pain behind her left temple made her wince. "Damn," she whispered, inhaling through her teeth. The pain burned for a few seconds, then subsided. Amanda chanced opening her eyes and moved her head from side to side, relieved that the pain was gone.

"Well, you can't have everything," she said. The small pains had started with her nightmares and she'd expected them to go away at the same time. When she was married to Neil she was sure the pains would disappear entirely.

Neil. She smiled again. Tonight was his bachelor party. Amanda had wanted to forgo tradition and make their own plans instead, but Neil had insisted. He'd been extremely hard to read these past few days and it had made her anxieties increase. But he'd assured her over and over again that he wanted to marry her and tomorrow was the day. Hallelujah! It seemed almost criminal that she could be this happy!

She went downstairs, looking around the empty house. Just a few hours and she and Neil would be together. Just a few more hours . . .

She was trying to decide how to spend the time when a delicious idea came to her: why not crash the bachelor party? If she just showed up for a few minutes Neil couldn't get too mad.

He might even be glad.

Greg locked the office door and tried to control his temper. Neil marrying Amanda! The guy had become completely irresponsible as a doctor and businessman. How could he be thinking of marriage?

Especially marriage to Amanda Howard.

Driving home, Greg's blood boiled with the injustice of it all. Poor Amanda. She'd looked so incredibly happy he'd been unable to shatter her dreams. Instead of blasting Neil like he should have when he'd heard the news, he'd let the matter slide. What a mistake! That marriage simply couldn't come off.

Not knowing exactly what he had in mind, Greg yanked the wheel around and headed for Neil's house. It was time they got a few things straight.

The lights in the living room were dim, the air smoky. Neil sat on the edge of the chair, drank down half his glass of scotch, looked at the glass, and realized he couldn't have another or it would be all over. He was an alcoholic; he knew it. But sometimes he could have a few drinks without needing another—gambling had replaced that obsessive need.

But not tonight.

Smoke from the woman's cigarette circled his head. "Well, are you gonna sit there all night, honey, or do you want some action?" Her hand slid over his thigh. "It's your money."

He finished his drink and set it down so hard on the coffee table it rolled off the edge and broke on the hardwood floor. Hazily, he wondered why he didn't care. "Less go upstairs," he slurred.

She helped him up from the couch. "Want another drink?"

Neil nodded and she poured him one as they headed for the stairs to his bedroom. "I'm geddin' married tomorrow," he said.

"Some bachelor party," the prostitute answered cynically. But it was all the same to her. As long as the drunk paid, anyway.

Amanda pulled into Neil's driveway, glancing

around in puzzlement. Shouldn't there be more cars? They hadn't gone somewhere else, had they? To some strip joint? Neil hadn't been too specific, she recalled.

She got to the front door and raised her hand to knock. Music drifted outside, soft and seductive. Thinking it was hardly appropriate for the raucous party she envisioned, she tried the knob. The door was unlocked.

Letting herself in, Amanda was about to call for him when she realized the record was skipping. Neil had just forgotten to turn it off.

So they did go someplace else, she thought, disappointed.

She switched off the turntable but still music played. From upstairs.

Amanda was about to mount the stairway when she heard soft laughter. Neil's laughter. Coming from his bedroom.

"No . . . don't do that," he said and laughed again.

The hairs on the back of her neck stood on end.

"Neil?" she called softly.

She crept silently up the stairway, heart pounding. She heard a woman's voice, crooning and moaning.

Amanda stood outside Neil's bedroom. For one cowardly instant she thought of turning and running; what she didn't know couldn't hurt her.

But she couldn't close her ears to the sounds issuing from behind his door. She twisted the knob.

One look was all it took. With a choked sob, she fled from the room.

"Amanda!"

She was down the stairs and out of the house. Her lungs felt on fire, as if they would burst from her pain. *Neil betrayed you!*

Her hands were shaking so badly she could barely insert the key in the lock. She fired the engine and backed out in a squeal of tires. A horn blared behind her. She ignored it and ground the gears, crying as she finally got the car moving forward, her foot pressed to the accelerator.

Greg swore, yanked the wheel to avoid hitting the car pulling out of Neil's driveway, and succeeded in knocking over the neighbor's garbage can. "Damn it all!"

The other car ground its gears and Greg glared at the driver. He saw a glimpse of blond hair and a tear-streaked face. *Amanda.*

"Amanda!" he called, but the car was racing away at a speed that made Greg's heart stop. Quickly he turned around and followed her.

She drove like a madwoman. It was all he could do to keep up with her. She had to wait for the wrought iron gates of her mansion to open and Greg caught her in time, but he couldn't get his car through. Helplessly he watched as the gates closed in front of him and she drove wildly up the curving drive, her tires slipping off the cement to spin in the rain-softened lawn more than once.

"Amanda!" Greg climbed out of his car and wrapped his hands around the iron bars. The taillights of her car disappeared around a huge hedge. Glancing around, he grabbed the bottom limb of a cherry tree that reached over the stone walls and began to climb.

* * *

Amanda felt hot inside, burning hot. She pressed the heels of her hands against her temples and shook violently. *Neil betrayed you!*

She unlocked the house and looked around unseeingly. Her emotions raged like white heat. She couldn't think.

She stood in the center of the room. Down the hall was the den. Charles's antique desk beckoned.

Amanda slowly walked toward it.

She opened the top drawer. The pistol was right where she'd left it. But it was unloaded. Remembering where the bullets were, she pulled out the bottom drawer.

Greg slid down the wall, his palms scraped and bleeding. *Amanda. Oh, Amanda. Whatever's wrong, please wait!* He'd never stopped to question his feelings for her; he'd never known what they were. But now, sensing her wild flight from Neil's house had been spurred by something terrible, his heart hammered with fear. What if she did something desperate before he could save her? He loved her, he realized. He had, almost from the first moment he'd seen her.

And now he was afraid he might lose her!

He ran until his lungs felt ready to explode. Rounding the hedge, he saw lights turn on in a corner room. "Amanda!" he yelled and ran to the front door. He jerked the handle but it was locked. She'd locked it.

She'd never handled a gun before except that one time she'd picked it up and pointed it, and then it had been unloaded. But now she was on fire and she wished she knew more about using one. She shook the bullets into the palm of her hand.

She set the bullets on the desk. Picking up the gun, she turned it over several times, seeing how it worked. Unlocking the chamber she methodically fed all six bullets inside. She was taking no chances. She snapped the chamber shut, then stiffened at the sound of breaking glass.

"Amanda!"

She heard the voice from somewhere down the hall, but it wasn't Neil's. Closing her eyes, she put the gun to her head.

"God! Amanda! *Don't!*"

Her finger was fumbling to find the trigger when she was thrown to the floor by another body. The gun skittered across the carpet. She struggled to reach it but hard arms held her down.

"Amanda, Amanda. What are you doing?" Greg Peters's voice said brokenly.

Slowly she focused on his face. His skin was stretched tightly over his cheekbones, his pallor white. Through her anguish she realized incredulously that this man truly cared what happened to her.

She opened her mouth but no sound came. Her eyes filled with tears and Greg cradled her close. "Oh, Amanda, don't scare me like that. I love you. I love you so much. All I want to do is protect you."

"Greg . . . ?"

"Shhh. Don't say anything. It'll be okay."

All the fight went out of her. She collapsed into a limp heap and felt his grip tighten. A choking sob wrenched itself free as she let his strength pull her away from the brink of destruction.

But inside she still hurt with a dull ache that seemed to have no end.

She hurt for Neil.

Chapter Ten

Love Conquers All

". . . if you so much as look at her again, I'll break your neck," Greg snarled at Neil, glaring at the bleary-eyed man seated at the kitchen table. "I was afraid to leave her last night. I called a nurse from the hospital to come stay with her to make sure she didn't try it again."

Neil's hand shook as he rubbed it over his unshaven jaw. "Look, Greg, it was all a misunderstanding—"

"Misunderstanding!" Greg exploded, slamming his fist down on the table. The plate of toast jumped and clattered and the coffee sloshed over the side of Neil's cup. "Damn it, Neil! She tried to kill herself!"

Neil pressed his lips together, head pounding. It was all he could do to keep from being sick. He wished Greg had had the decency to just leave him alone for a while, until he'd pulled himself together, but he'd just barged in at the crack of dawn making all kinds of ridiculous accusations. Amanda would never go to such lengths.

Would she?

With a shaking hand, he reached for his coffee. Good Lord, he wished he hadn't consumed so much alcohol last night. Maybe then he wouldn't have been so foolish as to hire a prostitute.

He winced at the memory. Too much booze and too much pressure. That's what had made him do it. He'd really wanted to marry Amanda; he still did. If only Greg would stop storming around his kitchen so he could get to the business of making up.

"Look, Greg—"

"No, you look. I'm putting you on notice. If you go anywhere near Amanda I'm calling the police."

"Where the hell do you get off?"

Greg stabbed a finger in front of his nose. "I'm trying to save the lady's life!" he roared.

"Sounds like you're trying for a piece of her yourself," Neil snarled back. "What about Susan? Maybe I should tell her about how the good Dr. Peters is looking for a—"

He never got to finish. Greg lunged at him so suddenly Neil was toppled from his chair. It was an unfair fight, over within seconds as Greg threw Neil to the floor.

Bells rang in his ears. He tried to struggle upward but felt too weak to move.

"I'm dead serious, Neil. Amanda's my patient now. You leave her alone."

Greg slammed out of the house before Neil could get his fury under control long enough to do more than swear. He pulled himself to his feet and leaned against the kitchen counter, panting. A pain shot through his ribs and he sucked air sharply through his teeth. Jimmy

Sentra's doing. And Greg had injured it again.

Thoughts of Sentra reminded Neil of what he'd lost. Amanda. All her money. All her love . . .

Shivering, he dialed her number, only to have the nurse Greg had hired answer and tell him Amanda wasn't able to come to the phone.

Neil thanked her and pressed the receiver, shaken. Could there be any truth to Greg's rantings? He vaguely remembered Amanda standing in the doorway, catching him in the most compromising way, but in the light of day he'd reasoned it had just been a manifestation of his own guilt. *Had she really been there?*

He had to talk to her.

With an effort he went upstairs, showered, shaved, and pulled himself together. "Don't blow this again," he said to his reflection. "This is your last chance."

It felt to Julie as if she were slowly awakening from an unbearable nightmare. David was dead, but life went on. This morning's incident had proved that: she'd felt movement inside her, a wave of motion that reminded her she couldn't give up. She was going to have a baby.

She thought of Doug and sadly realized there was no happy ending for them. They seemed destined to be one step out of sync, never able to fit their love into an imperfect world.

But she still had the baby to think of. And Bob. Though Doug owned her heart, Julie had new respect for her husband. Bob had been there for her during these trying times. He deserved more than a wife who pined for another lover.

Hearing the front door open and close

brought her out of her reverie. "Bob?" she called, bending over the rail at the upstairs landing.

Footsteps halted in the entryway. "It's Brooke."

Brooke! Julie banked down her distaste and descended the stairway. David loved Brooke, she reminded herself. That was reason enough to give the girl a second chance.

"We didn't know where you'd gone," Julie said, "or if you were coming back. I thought maybe you'd decided to . . ." Her voice trailed off in shock. Brooke was a wreck. Her face was gaunt, her cheekbones defined. Her hair was a tangled mess, her eyes lifeless, and her clothes looked as if they'd been slept in. *David's death did this to her*, Julie realized, and felt a pang of empathy.

Under Julie's startled gaze Brooke shifted uncomfortably. "Is Bob here?" she asked.

"He's at work."

"Then I'll come back later," she said, reaching for the door handle.

"Wait." Possessed by the need to make amends, Julie came over to her. "He's been worried about you. I don't know how many times he's asked me where you went. Neither of us knew."

"I was visiting friends," Brooke answered, her gaze sliding away.

"In Salem?"

"Yeah."

"I didn't know you knew anyone around here."

"What is this, the third degree?"

Her hostility reminded Julie of Brooke's true nature and she wondered if there were truly any way to reach her. "I was just asking," she said a trifle coolly. "For Bob."

It occurred to her all over again that her husband was unusually interested in Brooke. Though the last few weeks were hazy for Julie, Bob's concern for David's girlfriend had made an impression.

"Tell him I'm okay," she said. "I'll talk to him later."

"Any particular message?" Julie asked curiously.

Brooke narrowed her eyes, giving Julie a long, considering look. She seemed about to say something when they were both arrested by the sound of Bob's car coming up the drive. They were still standing by the front door when he walked in the house via the kitchen.

"Julie?" he called.

"In here." Julie hesitated, then said, "I'm with Brooke."

"Brooke?" Bob's footsteps quickened. He hurried from the back of the house, stopping a few feet away to stare at the younger woman as if he'd never seen her before. "Brooke, how are you? I've been so worried about you. Where have you been?"

"Around." Brooke regarded him warily, as perplexed as Julie by his sudden concern.

"What's going on here?" Julie asked. "Have I missed something?"

Instantly Bob turned his attention to her. "No, of course not." He ran a hand through his silvered hair and tried for a smile. It looked stiff and strained on his face. "You look better today, Julie," he said, giving her a quick squeeze.

She could feel how tensed up he was. Was

she crazy, or had something changed in his relationship with Brooke?

"I was just leaving," Brooke said.

"No!" Bob's arm fell from Julie's shoulders. "I, er, wanted to talk to you."

"About what?"

"A—letter came while you were away. Addressed to you. I opened it by mistake."

Brooke's brows furrowed. "A letter for me?"

"Yes. From your mother's solicitor." Bob licked his lip, then gently, while Julie looked on in disbelief, he slipped his arm around Brooke's waist, leading her toward the living room. "I'm sorry, Brooke. But your mother died several weeks ago. I've been frantic to tell you, but I didn't know how to reach you."

"My mother's dead?" she whispered dazedly.

Bob sat down with her on the couch, facing away from Julie. She stared at the back of their heads, thinking she didn't understand anything anymore.

"I know how terrible this is, coming so soon after David," Bob said soothingly, "and if there's anything I can do to help just say the word."

"I didn't know Brooke received a letter," Julie said.

"Just the other day." Bob flashed her a look over his shoulder. "I didn't mention it because you were so upset already."

Something flitted through Julie's memory. A letter? She was on the verge of recalling something important when the doorbell rang.

"Is Dad home?" Mary Anderson asked stiffly when Julie answered the door.

Julie looked at the petite young woman and inwardly sighed. Just deciding to make the most of her marriage wasn't going to help ease the situation with Bob's ex-wife and daughter. She wondered if she would ever make any inroads with Mary. "He's in the living room with Brooke."

"Brooke?"

"Brooke Hamilton. She was David's girlfriend. She's been staying with us."

Mary sidled in the direction of the living room. "Sorry about David," she said awkwardly, then hurried to see her father.

The sight that met her eyes was enough to send chills down her spine. Her father was actually holding this—this—Brooke person, comforting her.

". . . I found out in Adele's letter," he was saying in a low voice. "I never knew, Brooke. You've got to believe me. If I'd known I would have—" As if suddenly realizing he wasn't alone, Bob broke off and twisted around. "Mary!" he said in surprise.

"Hello, Dad." She circled the couch, standing in front of them. Who was this pathetic creature? "I couldn't wait any longer for you to come and visit me and Mom."

Her eyes focused harshly on Brooke's bent head. Bob cleared his throat. "Mary, this is Brooke Hamilton. Brooke, this is Mary." He paused. "My daughter."

Brooke lifted her head and brushed straggles of hair from her eyes. The look she gave her made Mary quail inside. It was as if she were judging her—and somehow found her lacking.

Julie had followed slowly after Mary. Now she entered the room and noticed the strange atmosphere brewing. Then she felt another move-

ment inside her and was diverted. She gently
rubbed her abdomen, aware she didn't really
care what was happening between Brooke and
Bob. It didn't matter anyway. There were much
more important things to think about. "I'm
going to start dinner," she said. "Think you
could stay, Mary?"

"No, I—well, yes. I'd like to."

"I'll set an extra plate."

As Julie left Bob cleared his throat, slowly
extricating himself from Brooke. She hadn't
been surprised to find out he was her father;
she'd already known. And miracle of miracles,
she seemed to accept him with no hard feelings!

He just wished he could continue the conversation without other ears listening—especially
Mary's. "How's Phyllis?" he asked, searching for
something to say.

"Doing better. I think she's finally accepted
the fact that you and Julie are married. She's
gotten over being sick all the time." Her eyes
drifted to Brooke.

As if on cue, Brooke rose and Mary instinctively felt on guard. She didn't like her. Didn't
like the way she made her feel.

For her part, Brooke was feeling much better
about herself. Learning about Adele's death had
been a shock, but not entirely unexpected.
Learning that Bob knew he was her father had
bowled her over. The most amazing thing of all
was that he seemed to really be concerned for
her welfare.

I'm not like my mother, she thought again,
but with more conviction. She could put the
past few weeks out of her mind and start
again—with her father.

"Are you from around here?" Mary asked in frosty tones.

"Ash Grove."

"Ash Grove? Where's that?"

Bob leapt to his feet, putting himself between Brooke and Mary in a way that warmed Brooke's heart and increased Mary's suspicions. "Let's all go in the kitchen. Julie's probably got dinner started by now."

Mary's face was set in stone and Brooke, enjoying the feel of having the upper hand, couldn't help stirring the pot a little bit. "Oh, Bob," she said, her face innocent. "I forgot to tell you. David's car conked out about three blocks down the street and I had to walk the rest of the way. I don't think it's salvageable."

"I'll call the service station to come haul it away and see if there's anything that can be done. In the meantime you can use my car. I'll borrow a truck from work."

"Dad!" Mary protested.

"What?"

"Well, why don't you just buy her a new car while you're at it," she said sarcastically.

Bob blinked. He turned to Brooke. "Is it really in that bad of shape?"

Brooke could have cheered. Mary's face turned dark red with anger. "I think so," she admitted dolefully.

"Well, we'll see what needs to be done in the morning," Bob said. "Come on." He ushered them toward the kitchen.

"Dad," Mary said through clenched teeth, grabbing his arm and holding him back. "What do you think you're doing?"

"I'm trying to get everyone to sit down at the

dinner table," he answered evenly.

"That's not what I meant and you know it. Can't you see what that girl's up to? She's angling for a new car!"

"You don't know anything about it." Bob stalked away from her.

"Oh, yeah? Maybe so. But I'm going to find out!"

Her vow fell on deaf ears as Bob strode out of sight. Brooke sauntered behind him, the smile on her face almost more than Mary could bear!

Who was this Brooke person and how had she weaseled her way into her father's affections? It was bad enough that she had to contend with Julie, but now Brooke, too?

Drawing up her chest, Mary followed after her father. She didn't know what was going on but she was bound and determined to find out. It might take some time, but in the end she would make sure she found out just who Brooke Hamilton was and what kind of strange hold she had on her father.

The gates to Amanda's house were shut tight. Neil could scarcely believe it. Why was she locking herself in? This was supposed to be their wedding day!

Uneasiness filled him but he pushed it away. He didn't want to even consider that Greg might have been telling the truth.

Neil started trekking toward the door at the far end of the wall, searching through his keys as he went. Getting inside was no problem, but facing Amanda was another proposition altogether. He already hurt all over. What was this talk going to do to his morale?

The door creaked open and Neil walked up the long cobblestone pathway to the side door. It was locked, too. He banged on it several times, swearing, and finally one of the most severe-faced women he'd ever encountered cracked it open the length of the chain lock.

He put on his best smile. "Good morning. I'm Neil Curtis. I'd like to see Amanda."

"She's not seeing anyone today."

"I'd like her to be the one to tell me that."

"I'm sorry, Dr. Curtis." The door edged shut.

Neil was instantly infuriated. So Greg had warned the old biddy about him! He tried to wedge his foot inside the door but the nurse kept shoving against it. With all his strength he rammed his shoulder hard against the panels. "Let me talk to Amanda or I'll break this down!" he roared.

"It's all right, Gladys," Amanda's soft voice drifted from inside. "I'll talk to him."

"But Dr. Peters said—"

"I know what he said. But I'll talk to Neil anyway."

Neil gave the nurse a baleful glare to which she just tightened her lips. She lifted her chin and marched from the room. "What a jailer," he muttered, his eyes turning to Amanda.

She was lovely, pale and fragile without a touch of makeup, a satin robe covering her soft shoulders.

"She only wants to help," Amanda said.

"Help how? What's wrong, sweetheart?" Neil took a step forward, reaching for her, but she backed away.

"What's wrong?" she whispered incredulously. "After last night you have the gall to ask me what's wrong?"

So she had been there. Neil's stomach dropped along with his already rock-bottom opinion of himself. He'd been terrible to her—used her even while he loved her. But that was all over now. All he wanted was to marry her, love her, make up for all the misery he'd caused her. "Amanda . . ."

"No, Neil. You can't just say 'I'm sorry' and expect me to believe you. I tried to kill myself last night because of you!"

"Amanda!"

"Didn't Greg tell you? He saved my life."

Shocked, Neil said, "I didn't believe him."

Amanda turned away, her chin quivering. "I catch you in bed with another woman the night before you and I are supposed to get married and you think I can just shrug it off?"

"No." He felt sick. Sick with himself.

"Why, Neil? Why? Why did you do it?"

"I felt scared," he said desperately. "I wasn't really ready for marriage."

"Then why did you ask me?"

"Because I love you."

For the first time Neil was truly sincere. He saw his future so clearly now. It would be nothing, an empty void without Amanda.

Why had he squandered her love?

"I don't believe you, Neil," she said, turning away. "I can't believe you."

"Amanda, I'll do anything to prove to you that I mean what I say. Please, don't shut me out of your life."

She shook her head. "I can't talk anymore right now," she whispered. "Please go."

"Amanda . . ."

She held up her hands. "Don't, Neil."

"If you need some time, I'll give it to you. But don't say it's completely over. Let me call you. Later. In a week or two. Please," he begged in anguish.

Her blue eyes swam with fresh tears. She couldn't trust him, but he looked so destroyed. "Maybe later . . ." she whispered.

Then she turned on her heel and ran out of the room.

Michael clumsily arranged the daisies and carnations in the cheap glass vase he'd purchased at the dime store. He set his creation on the table, pushed a few petals this way and that, then made a disgusted sound and gave up. *It's the thought that counts*, he reminded himself, recalling his mother's advice.

"Just be honest with her," Laura had said. "And show her you really care. *Tell* her you care. If Trish is the girl you think she is, she'll understand."

He'd believed his mother and had gained renewed faith. Why then, were his hands sweating so badly now?

The crunch of footsteps on gravel announced Trish's arrival. Michael held his breath. He hadn't seen her yet. He'd gone straight to work after catching the bus from Salem and hadn't had time to do more than buy the flowers and practice several different apologies.

The door opened. Trish walked inside, and stopped dead. "Michael," she said, her eyes widening.

"Now don't say anything else. Please. Not until you've given me a chance to explain. Okay?"

He pleaded with his eyes as much as his words. Trish, in a loose sweater and faded jeans, looked as young and vulnerable as he remembered her the first time he'd seen her. He wanted to reach out and hold her but forced himself not to.

Pulling out a chair, he inclined his head. "Come on. Sit down. I promise I won't touch you or do anything else to hurt you."

Trish's expression was hard to read, but after a brief hesitation she stiffly crossed the room and accepted the seat.

Michael sat down opposite her. "First, let me say I'm sorry." He smiled crookedly. "I'm sorry." When Trish didn't respond, he said quickly, "I was wrong to kiss you. I know how you feel about Jack—what he's put you through—and I shouldn't have been so stupid. It was a mistake."

Trish was staring down at her lap. Now she glanced up, quickly, before turning away. But her gaze landed on the straggly centerpiece he had created and he saw her swallow hard. "Why did you kiss me?" she asked unevenly.

"Because—because—" Michael's jaw worked, then he sighed. "Because I wanted to. I have for a long time."

"You've wanted to kiss me?"

"Oh, yeah." He laughed shortly. "That and a whole lot more."

Her shoulders tightened.

"Look . . ." Michael pushed back his chair and walked to the other side of the room, seating himself on the counter. This wasn't going at all like he wanted it to and he needed some distance from her. "Trish, I—since the moment I first saw you I had—feelings for you. Feelings I didn't want to tell you about because I knew you'd flip out. And then with the champagne and everything, the time just seemed right. I know it wasn't," he put in quickly. "You'd just been telling me about Jack, for Pete's sake! But I acted on impulse and well, you know the rest."

Trish plucked one of the carnations from the vase, fingering the ruffled white petals. After a long pause, she said, "I went over and visited my mother while you were gone."

"You did?"

"I didn't know who to turn to after you—after you left. She was great. Like she used to be."

"Really?" Michael was just relieved for the change of the subject. "Why? What happened?"

"She had a long talk with Jack. He's moved out. At least until they get things worked out. She told him . . ." Trish's voice broke off, her bottom lip beginning to quiver. "She told him that if he didn't leave me alone she was going to call social services and report him."

"But that's great," Michael said, sliding off the counter.

Trish nodded. "When she told me I was so relieved. I wanted to rush home and tell you. But you were gone."

Michael heard her soft condemnation and responded, "Trish, I wanted to be here for you, but I didn't think you wanted me. And I could hardly blame you. So, I went home for a while."

She looked up at him. "To your mother and Bill's?"

"We patched things up, sort of."

Biting her lip, she asked, "Does that mean you're moving back?"

"Not unless you kick me out."

"It's your apartment," she reminded him.

"Yeah, but you got it for me."

Hesitantly, her blue eyes looked up, searching his. Michael had never been particularly good at baring his soul, but he reached deep inside himself now, calling on a part of himself he hardly knew existed. "I don't want to leave. I care about you too much. I don't know much about love but this is as close as I've ever come. Hurting you just about killed me."

Trish's lips parted. Slowly, so exquisitely slowly that Michael thought he'd be deafened by his own heartbeats before she finally moved, she rose from her chair and came over to him. "Having you leave just about killed me," she said in a tremulous whisper. She put her arms around his neck and regarded him seriously. "You're my best friend."

His hopes sank. "That's all?" His arms lightly encircled her.

She ducked her head, afraid to give him a green light even though she was struggling with the same feelings. "I'm just afraid."

"Hey, I'm not exactly Mr. Confidence, here. How about if we take it one step at a time?"

"Think we could do that? And still live together?" She twisted her neck to see his expression.

"I'm willing to try." Trish smiled then and it was like a sunbeam cutting through shadows. Michael gave her a lopsided grin and lifted his hands in the air. "See? No pressure."

"Then I'm willing to try, too," Trish said shyly. "Let's start over as of today."

"As friends?"

Her cheeks flushed becomingly. "Yes. And maybe lovers, too. Someday."

Michael could have whooped for joy. There was still a chance for them, a good chance. A chance that hadn't been destroyed by her stepfather and his own miserable blundering.

"Someday," he repeated softly. They stared at one another for a long soulful moment, their trust in their eyes. Then he kissed her, lightly. The kind of kiss that sometimes happens between friends; the kind of kiss that sometimes leads to lovers.

And Trish kissed him back.

Susan waited in the darkened hallway. Her face was set and there was a grimness about her mouth that matched the howling wind outside. She'd tried with Greg—really tried. But in the end, just like everything else in her life, trying hadn't been good enough. She'd lost so much. Her first husband and his child. Her family and friends. Eric. The child she'd miscarried—the last she would ever be able to conceive.

And now Greg.

Where had he been last night? Who was he seeing? Did he really expect to come home in the wee hours of the morning and imagine she wouldn't have questions?

It was another woman. It had to be.

Her mouth curved into a cruel smile. Well, she wouldn't be the loser this time. No sirree. Greg was going to find out just what she was made of.

She couldn't wait until he came home.

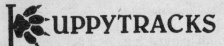